Also by K.A. Holt:

Rhyme Schemer

House Arrest

Knockout

Redwood and Ponytail

BenBee and the Teacher Griefer

Ben Y and the Ghost in the Machine

FIERCE ACROSS AMERICA
FIERCE ACROSS AMERICA!
Season 15
WHO'S AMERICA'S FIERCEST DANCER?
IT MIGHT BE YOU!

The Kids Under the Stairs

Jordan J

and the Truth About Jordan J

K.A. Holt

chronicle books · san francisco

Library of Congress Cataloging-in-Publication Data available.

ISBN 978-1-7972-0609-7

Manufactured in India.

Design by Jennifer Tolo Pierce.
Typeset in Fedra Mono, Cultura New, Air, GFY Ralston, FG Alex, FG Joe, and Karmatic Arcade.
Illustrations by K.A. Holt.

10 9 8 7 6 5 4 3 2 1

Chronicle Books LLC
680 Second Street
San Francisco, California 94107

Chronicle Books—we see things differently. Become part of our community at www.chroniclekids.com.

For the real Mo,

whose questions always give me answers.

THE HART TIMES

★ ★ ★ *JORDAN J'S BOO-YAH REPORT #1!* ★ ★ ★

Here's the thing: The Hart Rocketeers dance team COULD be good. They could even be GREAT. But they won't be good or great until every dancer dances like Casey Price.

There are a few other dancers who are pretty good, too, but just like Veronica Verve says in *Fierce Across America* (the best dance competition show in the history of all time): Good is fine, but electric is fierce.

Why don't ALL the Hart Rocketeers dance like they're electrified?

I have a theory: My theory is that Ms. Masterson, the dance team coach, would not recognize exciting and electric dance moves even if she was struck by lightning and that lightning gave HER some exciting and electric moves.

★ ★ ★ ★ ★

The Hart Rocketeers will never beat the Freshwater North Fire 'Canes unless Ms. Masterson can find some energy in her dance routines. There's only so much Casey Price can do for a whole dance team, you know? Until Ms. Masterson steps it up, the Rocketeers will never be better dancers than even the worst dancers on *Fierce Across America*. And those dancers are clown music dancers.

BOO-YAH REPORT OUT!

Dance like EVERYONE'S watching,

Jordan J

Jordan,
See me in my office before Newspaper Typing Club today.
—Ms J

★★★★★

THE HART TIMES

★ ★ ★ JORDAN J'S ★ ★ ★

To Jordan J: dumb

~~BOO-YAH~~ REPORT #2!

Here's the thing: You stink!

Here's the thing: The Hart Rocketeers dance team wrote a lot of Letters to the Editor about how hard they work and about how much they did not like my Boo-Yah Report #1 and about how much energy they could each bring as they practice their high kicks straight into my behind.

And so they would like an apology. WHERE IS IT ???

And so I will apologize for using words and a tone that wasn't as professional as it should have been, according to Ms. J, our Newspaper Typing Club faculty advisor, and Ms. Masterson, the dance team coach.

THIS IS NOT AN APOLOGY!

And everyone on the dance team, dingus!

I have a theory: Even though I will and am and do apologize, that apology will not make the Hart Rocketeers better dancers than the Freshwater North Fire 'Canes or better than the *Fierce Across America* clown music dancers.

★ ★ ★ ★ ★

WE HAVE A THEORY THAT YOU STILL NEED A SWIFT KICK IN THE [donkey drawing]

What is that, Beverly?

Only fierce energy and better dance routines will do that.

Please do not energetically kick the dance critic in the butt for telling the truth, as telling the truth is my job (that I get paid zero dollars for), but do because I love dancing and I want the Hart Rocketeers to smash those smug Fire 'Canes with the fierce energy rockets are known to have.

So there.

It's a Donkey!!

BOO-YAH REPORT OUT!

Oh. Sorry.

Dance like EVERYONE'S watching.

Jordan J

YEAH. JORDAN J NEEDS A KICK IN THE DONKEY.

Jordan,
we received many letters like this today. Please meet me in my office before Newspaper Typing Club today. -Ms J

★★★★★

14 DAYS

TO *FIERCE ACROSS AMERICA* PRELIMS*

***Zero** days for me because the closest city hosting auditions is all the way down near Miami and Mom and Dad said no way they would drive down there even though Mom totally could now that she has no job and Dad also totally could because his job is flexible which means he sleeps late and does all the grocery shopping, but no one will drive me and there's no money for a hotel anyway.

MO'S OFFICE

I look up at Mo, who is sitting across from me with her notebook on her lap and her glasses on the tip of her nose and a little bit of something stuck to the side of her mouth like maybe she had a piece of cake for lunch.

I take the pencil out of my mouth so I can ask:

Did you have a piece of cake for lunch?

Mo points at the list/letter I'm writing and lifts her eyebrows.

Are you finished already?

She always answers my questions with questions, which is a thing I am not a huge fan of, if I'm being honest, and I'm always honest because my face and my mouth don't let me *not* be honest.

I still don't really understand what I'm doing?

I make my eyebrows match Mo's eyebrows.

I can't write a list of things I'm excited about if there's nothing I'm excited about?

I'm saying everything like a question so that I can answer all of Mo's questions with a question, too.

Mo scratches her cheek and accidentally knocks off her glasses, but they don't hit the floor because they're attached to a chain, so they just swing down and bonk into another pair of glasses hanging around her neck.

Hey, Mo?
Why are you wearing TWO pairs of glasses?

That one's a real question, but she doesn't answer me. She just points to my list-of-nothing and says,

How about three more minutes to finish up?

Of all people, Mo should know that I can't finish *anything* in three minutes. I mean, the whole point of coming to see Mo is so I can tell her all the ideas and thoughts and worries in my head and that way I can hopefully make a little extra room in my brain for other things like remembering to do my homework and/or remembering how to be calm and happy and/or just having three minutes of not thinking about anything at all, just floating in my brain space and breathing deep.

Maybe if Mo had that awesome dictation software we got for Newspaper Typing Club so everyone can write their articles with their voices—except for Ben B, who types faster than he can talk, which, what even IS that superpower?—maaaaybe then I could finish this in three minutes. I don't know.

I hand my list to Mo when she tells me to.

That was a fast three minutes.

IMPORTANT THINGS ON MY MIND: REQUESTED BY MO: A NUMBERED LIST OF NUMBERS BY JORDAN J

1. 0 answers from you, Mo, about why you are wearing 2 pairs of glasses with necklaces attached to them
2. 0 answers from you, Mo, about whether you had cake for lunch, and if you might have some left over that I could share and/or steal
3. 0 countdown days to *Fierce Across America* auditions because it's too far away and no one will drive me there
4. 0 dollars to pay for a hotel room even if someone WOULD drive me there, which no one will
5. 0 ideas why Mom and Dad call saving money *belt*-tightening? Why isn't it called *money*-tightening?
6. 8 dance moves for 1 super-sweet dance routine that I can never show to Veronica Verve, THE . . . NUMBER . . . 1 . . . FIERCEST . . . DANCE . . . COMPETITION . . . JUDGE . . . OF . . . THE . . . CENTURY, because 0 people will drive me to auditions

7. ???? days until Mom gets a new job that makes tons of extra money so maybe next time *Fierce Across America* has auditions even sort of nearby someone will drive me and there will be extra money for a hotel room if the auditions are far away

8. ???? days until Mom gets a new job with extra-good health insurance so that I can see you every time I need to and not just every now and then or whatever the plan is now, I forget

9. ???? lists before I actually think of something fun to look forward to

10. maybe that's everything?

11. oh, wait. 0 dollars for watercolors for the old-lady art class I'm taking with Javi

Peace out,
Jordan J

PS: Maybe I need some lists of things to not forget, too.

Mo looks at my list and then back at me.

> *Can you explain to me what your body is doing right now, Jordan?*

I look down at my body all scrunched up in a ball in this itchy orange chair.

Can't she tell this is the Pork Chop Protection Ball™ everyone learns in the Sandbox tutorial? For when you accidentally walk into an Infinite Pork Chop Replicator and pork chops fly at your avatar from every direction, and unless you're wearing armor you have to curl up in a ball to protect your squishy parts in order to survive?

I mean, duh.

I guess I could explain that I'm using the Pork Chop Protection Ball™ to protect myself, even though this is real life and not a video game, because my own feelings are coming at me just like they're an uncontrolled stream of computer-generated pork chops.

But I don't really need to explain that to her, do I? I mean *everyone* plays Sandbox, even my teacher-librarian Ms. J, who has finally learned how to use a pickax without chopping off anyone's arms.

If *Ms. J* legit plays Sandbox, then Mo must play, too, because she's equally as cool as Ms. J. So she should definitely be able to recognize a simple—

Jordan?

I blink.

I look at Mo.

I didn't even realize I'm doing that thing where I stare off into the distance while I think about a lot of stuff. Sometimes I do the opposite and I say a lot of things while my brain stares off into the distance.

Neither one of those things is great, but at least Mo helps me understand that that is just how I process the world.

Process is Mo's word for it.
I call it *Jordan-ing.*

Sorry.
Am I Jordan-ing again?

Mo smiles and tilts her head to the side so she can . . . I don't know . . . look at me sideways? I squeeze my arms around my knees even harder so that the itchy chair doesn't touch my elbows.

I'm protecting my squishy parts, Mo.

Mo nods and writes something in her notebook.

I look over at the clock.

5 minutes until Mo smiles at me like she does just before she says, *Well it looks like we're out of time.*

4 minutes and 30 seconds until Mo says, *Can you send your Mom in on your way out?*

3 minutes until I'm waiting for Mom in Mo's lobby.

2 minutes until Mom won't be making an appointment with Mo so I can talk to her next week.

1 minute until—

Jordan?

Sorry. I'm Jordan-ing a lot today, huh?

That's perfectly understandable.
Can you send your Mom in?

Yeah.

Thanks.

Mo smiles at me in that way she does where I want to smile back but also cry a little bit because it feels so nice to know someone who kind of understands my brain.

Today I also want to cry a little bit because I don't know when I'll be back. When I walk out of this quiet office I'm afraid the world will feel especially . . . a lot . . . because no one out there will even kind of understand my brain.

Well, actually, maybe Ben B and Ben Y and Javier and Ms. J understand my brain a little bit. Or at least it doesn't bother them like it does some people. They don't care if I'm Jordan-ing, just like I don't care about all their Ben B-ing or Ben Y-ing or Javier-ing or Ms. J-ing.

Bye, Jordan.
Until next time . . .

I look away from the unfocused future and back at Mo's smile.

I like that she emphasized the word *until*, like next time is definitely happening sometime.

I also like that she didn't say it like a question.

I spin in a quick pirouette, catch myself after one turn, do a quick pop-and-lock worm with my arms that ends with me pointing at Mo and saying,

Can't wait to see youuuuu . . . MO often!

Mo's eyes widen for a second and she laughs for an even quicker second and I love it when I can surprise Mo and make her laugh, even when she tries to hide it, and even when she doesn't understand she's supposed to catch my pop-and-lock arm worm and send it back to me.

THINGS THAT SHOULD LIVE ON THIS PAPER INSTEAD OF IN MY BRAIN: A LIST BY JORDAN J

1. remember to finish my Boo-Yah Report #3 for the newspaper
2. probably a lot of remembering to do a lot of other homework, idk
3. remember to bring my lunch to school now that Dad is making it every morning because of the money belt-tightening
4. remember to tell Dad I don't like hot dogs wrapped in tin foil in my lunches
5. remember to tell Dad to stop putting pickled peaches in plastic lunch bags in my lunch because even though they taste good, they look really really really really gross
6. other stuff
7. remember to go to Newspaper Typing Club, which I think might be right now

SCHOOL*

JORDAN!
JORDAN!
JORDAN!
JORDAN!

Ben Y's shoulder slams into the side of my face because she's waving a piece of paper and running and doesn't see my back-pack on the floor by the computer tables and probably this is why every grown-up in my life is always yelling at me to *move your backpack under your desk, Jordan, stop leaving your backpack in the middle of the doorway, Jordan, get your bag out of the aisle, kid.*

Ow!

She slugs me in the shoulder even though she's the one who crashed into ME.

You, ow!
Look!

Ben Y waves the paper at me and she's breathless and smiling and I like how the light from the library skylight shines on her head and makes all the tiny shaved hairs sparkle like glitter.

*Technically *after* school. In the library, for Newspaper Typing Club.

I take the paper and look at it and once all the letters stop jumping around like tiny fruit flies, they settle in place and I rearrange them so they make sense and—

WHAT!

The search is ON to discover TEN fierce dancers for our groundbreaking 15th season! Prepare your best moves and see if YOU can make it past Prelims. Get to Callbacks and you're only one stage away from Finals. Then? BOOM. Watch out Veronica Verve and Mae Michaelson—

WHO'S AMERICA'S FIERCEST DANCER?
IT MIGHT BE **YOU!**

Due to overwhelming interest, we've added **new** cities to our audition list. Your city, FRESHWATER, FLORIDA, is one of them. We will see you THIS Saturday!

10 SECONDS LATER, STILL AT SCHOOL

I yell:

What day is it today?!

Ms. J yells from behind the checkout area:

The twenty-third!

I yell back:

What DAY, though?

Ms. J points to the TODAY'S DATE sign hanging behind her at the checkout desk and yells:

Tuesday!

And then Ben Y and I both do some counting on our fingers and yell at the same time:

ONLY SIX DAYS!

*Right here in town! No road trip or hotel necessary! Whaaat!!!!!

A SECOND LATER, STILL AT SCHOOL

Ben B leans over my shoulder and looks at the paper.

> *Can you believe it?*
> *The front office sent down a stack of papers,*
> *announcements and things—*
> *stuff we might want for the* Hart Times*—*
> *and* half *of it has already* happened.

I can barely hear him.

I'm too busy spinning in circles and shouting out questions like I'm one of those sparking fireworks that ping-pong down the street if you aren't careful.

> *WHY AM I ONLY FINDING OUT ABOUT THIS NOW?*
> *HOW DID I NOT KNOW THEY ADDED*
> *FRESHWATER TO THE AUDITION CITIES??*
> *HOW WILL I BE ABLE TO CREATE A PERFECT*
> *TEN OUT OF TEN OUTSTANDING TWO-MINUTE*
> *DANCE ROUTINE IN ONLY*
> *SIX DAYS?*
> *HOW—*

Ms. J hollers something about volume which is funny because she hollers it from across the library.
I try to lower my spinning fireworks voice.

How—

I don't get a chance to ask my next *how*, though, because Ms. J floats over like a fast-moving stingray, and she says,

HOW do you explain all this shouting when the rule is No Talking During the Typing Part of Newspaper Typing Club?

Ben Y flops into a seat and sighs.

I liked it better when it was just a secret Sandbox club that we called Typing Club.

Ben B nods and looks off into the distance, almost like he's Jordan-ing.

Yeah.
Back when we all were in the same class.
And I tricked Ms. J into playing Sandbox with us.
And made her love it!

He snorts out a laugh and Ben Y turns her sigh into a laugh, too, and Ms. J says,

First of all, no one tricked me into anything.
I knew what I was doing.

Javier gives her the look we all want to give her and she blows out some breath almost like a fart noise in response.

SECOND, Newspaper Typing Club is just as fun,
if not more fun.
And *more rewarding.*

She nods once, puffs up her chest, and snaps twice before any of us can say anything else.

Tick
tock,
I'll spot you ten minutes for Sandbox, you y'alls,
because, yes, I love it, too,
but then *we have got to get to work.*
The Hart Times *doesn't write itself.*

Ben B, Ben Y, Javier, and I all say: *The* Hart Times *doesn't write itself!* at the same time Ms. J says it because she says it allllllllllll the time, even though we know a school newspaper can't write itself—that would be really weird.

< Newspaper Typing Club Chat >

jajajavier:): You ready for later?

JORDANJMAGEDDON!!!!: Yes! My brain might be thinking about super sweet dance moves for my FAM tryout, but the rest of me

CHAT INFRACTION

JORDANJMAGEDDON!!!!: will be ready to hang out with you and learn some super sweet painting moves

JORDANJMAGEDDON!!!!: side note: I still don't have my own paint. Sorry.

JORDANJMAGEDDON!!!!: Can I keep borrowing yours?

jajajavier:): Sure. I don't mind.

jajajavier:): even when you don't rinse your brush

jajajavier:): browple is my new favorite color.

0BenwhY ENTERS CHAT

0BenwhY: What is a browple??

JORDANJMAGEDDON!!!!: brown and purple mixed together!

jajajavier:):

PlanetSafeAce: 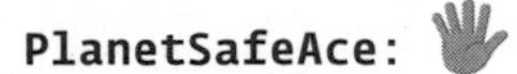

jajajavier:): That was actually for Jordan.

PlanetSafeAce: I know, but he was too slow.
PlanetSafeAce: Never leave a high five hanging.

BenBee: Never leave a high five hanging.

0BenwhY: Never leave a high five hanging.

JORDANJMAGEDDON!!!!: Never leave a high five hanging.

jajajavier:): Anywaaaay. Can't wait to learn new watercolor tricks today. Wooo!

JORDANJMAGEDDON!!!!: Javi, you know I don't like learning things when I'm not in school.

JJ11347: Har, har.
JJ11347: Please don't say that right in front of me, a person who is a huge fan of learning.

JORDANJMAGEDDON!!!!: Sorry, Ms. J.
JORDANJMAGEDDON!!!!: learning is the best i love it learning is great hooray for learning yay

JJ11347:

0BenwhY: Excuse me, but this isn't the Javi and Jordan Social Hour.
0BenwhY: Aren't we supposed to be, you know . . . *playing a video game here*? 🙄
0BenwhY: Building stuff . . . making potions . . .
0BenwhY: watching Ms. J get ejected for her chat infractions . . .

BenBee: Hello, are you Ben Y-splaining how Sandbox works???
BenBee: We're ALL experts, you know.

0BenwhY: I'M BEING SARCASTIC.

JJ11347: In Ben Y's defense, we HAVE all agreed to play Sandbox as a way to decompress and connect before sta

CHAT INFRACTION

jajajavier:): 💀 ja ja ja

0BenwhY: 👵

JJ11347: Yes, yes, right on cue.
JJ11347: I'm old, chat infractions haunt my dreams, and you're all hilarious.

0BenwhY: Seriously, though.

0BenwhY: Javi and Jordan you need to make your plans AFTER Sandbox.

0BenwhY: Our time is already almost up and we haven't built anything.

PlanetSafeAce: I, for one, have neither decompressed, nor felt connected.

PlanetSafeAce: 🤷🏾‍♀️ 😄

JJ11347: Speaking of After Sandbox . . .

JJ11347: Javier and Jordan, you both need to turn in your articles when we log off.

JORDANJMAGEDDON!!!!: Oooh, yeah. About that . . .

JJ11347: Stop. Nope. UH-UH. 😖

JJ11347: Due two days ago, Jordan.

JJ11347: And you know I have to approve it this time.

JJ11347: TWICE I let you get away with turning it in so late I couldn't approve before it printed.

JJ11347: TWICE I have been burned.

JJ11347: Never again.

JJ11347: And I need it NOW or there will be no Boo-Yah Report in this edition.

JORDANJMAGEDDON!!!!: Can I use that magic dictation software?

JORDANJMAGEDDON!!!!: If I can, then I can be done super soon.

JORDANJMAGEDDON!!!!: Probably.

JORDANJMAGEDDON!!!!: I mean, it's basically already written.

JORDANJMAGEDDON!!!!: In my brain.

BenBee: IT'S ALREADY TWO DAYS LATE AND YOU HAVEN'T EVEN STARTED???

JJ11347: What your editor said 👆

JJ11347: Thank you, Ben B.

JORDANJMAGEDDON!!!!: SORRYYYYYYYYYYYY

BenBee: Dude. You don't have to shout.

BenBee: Just get it done, ok?

BenBee: I'll help you get the dictation software working.

JJ11347: Okay, everyone, since we aren't building anything and clearly deadlines are being ignored like a mid

CHAT INFRACTION

jajajavier:): 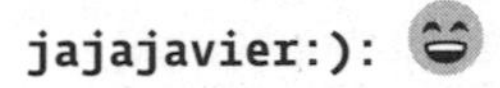

PlanetSafeAce: 💀

0BenwhY: 👵

JJ11347: Shut.

JJ11347: It.

JJ11347: Down.

BenBee HAS EXITED CHAT

jajajavier:) HAS EXITED CHAT

0BenwhY HAS EXITED CHAT

JORDANJMAGEDDON!!!! HAS EXITED CHAT

JJ11347 HAS EXITED CHAT

STILL AT NEWPAPER TYPING CLUB, IN THE LIBRARY, AFTER SCHOOL*

> *Hello, hi, yes, nice to meet you, my name is Jordan J, and I am the best and fastest newspaper article writer in the whole world.*

I frisbee the printout of my article onto the table in front of Ben B, who looks up from his keyboard and puts on his *I Am the Editor of the Newspaper and You Are Not* expression, which is kind of a mix of someone who thinks he's fancy but also needs to fart.

> *Wellllll, you* are *still two days late. So I don't know about fastest—*

I interrupt him by blowing all the air out of my body in a very slow fart noise that I aim directly at his face, fluttering his bangs and making him frown but laugh at the same time.

> *Gross!*
> *Stop!*
> *Your breath smells like Funyuns and M&M's.*

I smile.

*After the typing part of Newspaper Typing Club, which is really just code for playing Sandbox with Ms. J.

That's because I ate Funyuns and M&M's for lunch.
You're lucky I did not eat that wrinkly hot dog Dad packed for me.

Ben B uses my article to fan the air in front of his nose.

I'll see if I can fit this in.
Even though it's late.

Ace looks up over their computer monitor, laughing loudly.

Fitness pizza in my mouth!

Ace stops laughing and looks up at the ceiling, thinking.

Or, I guess . . .
Fitness article in my paper?
Hey, anybody writing a fitness article?
That's actually a good idea.

Ms. J yells from her office:

That IS a good idea, Ace!
And there better be ZERO people eating pizza in my library!

Ben B, please bring me Jordan's article.
STAT.

Ace slides back behind their monitor. I peek over mine and offer a thumbs-up.

Jokes are tricky, but at least you tried.

Ace doesn't say anything.

I slide back down into the seat behind my monitor.

Wait.

Shouldn't *I* be in Ms. J's office with Ben B and *my* article?

Ben Y, who has been weirdly quiet all day, leans around her monitor and says,

You better get in there.

As if she can read my mind.

You don't want to offend the entire dance team for the third issue in a row.

She shakes her shaved head at me and tries to look serious but her eyes give her away.

I moonwalk to Ms. J's office, adding some shrugs that work as a response to Ben Y, and also add a little extra pop to my moves.

Maybe they'll finally start listening to me.

Ben Y shrugs back at me to match my own shrug pops, and says cheerfully,

Doubt it!

THE HART TIMES

★ ★ ★ *JORDAN J'S* ★ ★ ★

BOO-YAH REPORT #3!

Here's the thing: Those Freshwater North Fire 'Canes? The only dance team the Hart Rocketeers can't seem to beat? Like *ever*?

They're not even that good, you y'alls.

They're just pretty okay.

So why do they keep beating us every year, over and over?

I have a theory: Until the Rocketeers coach, Ms. Masterson, starts using super-sweet dance moves like:

* baby freezes
* leaps of any kind
* sharp pops of heads and arms instead of sad, droopy not-pops of heads and arms
* etc.

the Fire 'Canes will keep using their hotttt dance moves to burn up any chance the Hart Rocketeers have at blasting off to district finals.

That's right.

The Fire 'Canes might not be great, but they are at least interesting to watch. Also, they are very energetic and don't seem to hate to be on the stage. Not that every

Better way to phrase this?

I would hope not!

★ ★ ★ ★ ★

Rocketeer seems to hate being on the stage, I'm just saying if ALL the Rocketeers had the same fierce energy as Casey Price, team captain, and if Ms. Masterson thought up some dance moves that are for human dancing and not turtle dancing, then . . . ? what is turtle dancing?

Mind.

Blown.

~~Exploding head emoji.~~ cut

Dear Ms. Masterson: Try watching Seasons 5 through 10 of *Fierce Across America*. write out numbers

Veronica Verve teaches D'Andre some *super*-extra-sweet dance moves, and then he adds his own spin on some of them, and boo-yah, they make serious dance magic.

If the Hart Rocketeers had, like, 67% of that serious dance magic, the Fire 'Canes would fizzle out for sure.

Dance like EVERYONE'S watching,

Jordan J

Be careful of your tone. Try again, and work on being more helpfully constructive (with a respectful tone).
-Ms J

OLD-LADY ART CLASS*

Javier is very very very excited about old-lady art class today and I wish I could also be that excited, because it's fun to be excited about something *with* someone else, and not just *next* to some-one else.

Buuuuut . . .

I only said yes to taking this class because I thought Javi was right that it would be fun to have some bro time together somewhere that's not school and not in a video game. And I liked that he chose me to be his friend to want to do that with.

Buuuuut . . .

He didn't say that it was THREE TIMES A WEEK for SIX WEEKS, NO REFUNDS, even if your mom asks really nice for that refund and explains that no one reads the fine print because everyone is busy and she could really use that money back.

Annnnnnd . . .

*It's actually called Watercolor Basics, and it's at Freshwater Community Center, and I don't think Javier realized that it would be me and him and eight old ladies learning Watercolor Basics from our teacher, who is not old but also not young either. I like all the ladies. They say swears sometimes and laugh a lot and sometimes bring snacks.

Now I have to REALLY LOVE old-lady art class, not just because of bro time with Javier, but also because Mom's cheeks got really pink after that lady said, *No refunds,* and then Mom growled, *You better love this stinkin' class, Jordan,* but then right after that she sighed and said, *Sorry, I mean, I know you'll love it, and I'm so glad you're doing something fun that's not on a screen.*

Soooooo . . .

I have some pressure to be excited.

Also, all the old ladies are really good artists and so is Javier and I feel pressure about that, too.

Maybe I can paint out the new dance routine I'm thinking about for FAM auditions in six days.

The teacher who wants us to call her by her first name, which is a mystery name I can never remember, walks by and leans over the table that Javi and I share with Carol and Carole with an E. She makes cooing sounds, which might be the sounds of the birds Carol and Carole are painting, or might be the sounds she makes when she likes something?

Kat!

Yes?

Oh, sorry, did I say that out loud?
I just remembered your name.

The Carol(e)s snort-laugh and one of them winks at me and I look down at my not-bird and wonder, *how* many more of these classes do we have?

Kat leans over to talk about fancy watercolor stuff with Javi and Javi actually drops the hoodie part of his hoodie so he can lean in closer to match the angle of Kat's lean and their leaning heads make a triangle over Javi's bird and wait a second. Wasn't it supposed to be MY turn after the Carol(e)s?

I've only seen Javier take the hoodie part of his hoodie off, like, three times ever. Usually, he's tightening it and trying to hide his face.

He nods and smiles and laughs at whatever Kat just said and I'm starting to think maybe Javi doesn't care that much if I'm here with him at all.

BRO TIME AT OLD-LADY ART CLASS

Javi, how did you already paint such a good bird? my bird looks like:

HEY! DON'T WRITE ON MY BIRD!

I MEAN ME! TWEET!

Sorry. Can you show me how to paint a dancing bird?

BUT... DO YOU LIKE KAT?

WHO?

THE TEACHER! OF THIS CLASS!

Ohhhh. Kat I didn't know Cat could have a K. She seems fine I guess

YEAH SHE'S COOL.

You KNOW YOU CAN TALK TO ME AND NOT WRITE ON MY BIRD, RIGHT?

Yesssss sss!

FAM TRYOUTS IN 6 DAYS!!!!

IF I MAKE A LIST OF ALL MY CLASSES AT SCHOOL AND THEN CROSS THEM OFF AS THE DAY GOES ON AND ON AND ON, WILL THAT MAKE THE DAY GO BY FASTER: A TEST BY JORDAN J

1. homeroom
2. math
3. ELA
4. ~~lunch~~
5. ~~PE~~
6. ~~what's the class where you learn about where countries live and what rivers they have? That one~~ Geography!
7. ~~PRIDE~~
8. ~~earth science~~
9. ~~after school: Newspaper Typing Club~~

10. Watch dance team practice juuuust in case anyone has good dance moves I can use for my FAM routine!

ANSWER: No

THE NEXT DAY, AFTER SCHOOL

AGAIN, LADIES.

[whistle]

IF YOU THINK YOU'RE SWEATING NOW,
JUST IMAGINE HOW YOU'LL FEEL WHEN
WE GET DROWN-BURNED BY THE FIRE
'CANES IN DISTRICTS.

[whistle whistle whistle]

DO IT AGAIN UNTIL IT'S . . .

[whistle]

. . . RIIIIIIIIIIIIGHT.

[long whistle]

I peer through the dusty dirty window on the broken back door of the gym.

Sure, I could go inside the gym to watch the Rocketeers practice, but my article came out today and even though it was very helpful and had several constructive ideas, a girl in the math hallway yelled at me, *You better watch it, Jordan J. Ms. Masterson is ready to rip you to shreds and turn your guts into new shoes!*

Yikes.

[whistle] [whistle] [whistle]

I duck down so Ms. Masterson doesn't see me and try to turn my guts into jazz shoes.

DROP IT LOW, LADIES!

[whistle]

NOT LIKE THAT! THAT WAS TERRIBLE!

[whistle]

DO IT AGAIN!

Casey Price does it again, and she is so super good at dropping it low. I hope she doesn't want to make shoes out of my guts, too. I always say nice things about her in my articles because she really makes everything look easy. She doesn't wobble when she drops it down low, and the rest of her moves are both electric AND smooth, just boom, like splitting your body practically in half is the easiest thing in the world.

In fact, it seems so easy, I test out dropping it low right here, right now, and it turns out it *isn't* as easy as Casey Price makes it look, just like I thought.

My head wobbles forward, banging into the metal door like I just rang a gong—a big one like they have in the back of the band room and only use for very important band shows, like eighth-grade graduation.

HEY!

[whistle]

Uh-oh.

[whistle whistle whistle whistle]

YOU!

[long whistle]

I rub my head where it banged into the door and peek through the window and wow, Ms. Masterson is a really fast walker. She pushes hard on the door, opening it so fast I have to jump back so my head doesn't gong into it again.

WHO ARE YOU?
ARE YOU A SPY FOR FRESHWATER NORTH?

I back up, hands raised, heart smashing around in my chest.

I'm Jordan J!
No relation to Ms. J the librarian who is also named

Jordan J!
I'm not a spy!
I–

A Rocketeer with her hands on her hips and a very not-nice look on her face interrupts me and says in a loud voice,

That's the kid who keeps writing newspaper articles about how terrible we are.
He called us . . . bad dancers.

There's a low *ooooooh* that rises up from the rest of everybody in the gym. Now a whole lot of Rocketeers have their hands on their hips and are looking at me in a very not-nice way.

Ms. Masterson looks at me like she wishes she could shoot actual fire out of her eyes and into my face.

You.

It seems like she wishes she could *breathe* fire, too. All over me.

How DARE you–

I wave my hands around because I don't know what else to do with them.

No, no, no . . . I didn't mean anything I wrote in a BAD way!

I want to HELP.
I promise!
I want you all to be the best dance team in the whole state.
The whole world.
The whole universe!

The Rocketeers are advancing through the gym toward me and I'm a little worried they're not hearing the words I'm saying.

I talk louder.

I was offering advice!
Trying to help!
Trust me!
I'm a good dancer!
I know stuff!
About dancing, I mean.
I totally do!
I dance all the time!
I'm always thinking of new and cool ways to dance!
And to connect dance moves into routines that are like . . .

I make a *zzzzzz* noise and flutter my fingers through the air like I'm lightning.

Everyone stares at me.

Some of the girls snort very, very quietly.

My brain is fully Jordan-ing now—the kind where it peaces out and my mouth keeps talking—and I don't even try to stop it.

> *I'm telling you, if everyone—especially Casey Price—learned how to do super-sweet dance moves instead of old boring ones, the Hart Rocketeers could probably definitely beat those Freshwater North Fire 'Canes for the first time ever.*

Ms. Masterson's eyes narrow and her mouth opens, but before she can say anything, Casey Price cocks a hip to the side, lifts her chin in my direction, and marches closer to the doorway that Ms. Masterson is blocking with her electrically angry, turquoise-tracksuit-covered self.

Casey Price looks at me over Ms. Masterson's shoulder.

> *Like what KIND of super-sweet dance moves? Put your moves where your mouth is, Mr. Boo-Yah Report.*

A few other Rocketeers inch forward so they can peek around Ms. Masterson, too. Some of them go, *Yeah!*

I don't say anything and I don't wait for anyone else to say anything, I just . . .

BAM

. . . drop it down low two times back-to-back, superfast, like my whole body is a heartbeat, and even though my moves are not as smooth as Casey Price's, on the second drop I push hard with my bouncing legs up into a backflip which accidentally turns into more of a diagonalflip, but that's okay because I land on my side in the grass and put my hand under my chin and smile big like I'd planned to do that the whole time.

Ms. Masterson closes her mouth.

Ms. Masterson crosses her arms.

Ms. Masterson does not blow her whistle.

More Rocketeers appear behind her, standing on their tiptoes to watch me.

I leap up from the grass and drop it low again, but this time I swing one arm over my head and drop my other arm to the ground and make up a SUPER-sweet move that's like a baby freeze and a drop-it-low Frankensteined together. Easier than a backflip, and almost as outstanding. Eight out of ten, at least.

I wonder if this is what it's like to dance for your life on *Fierce Across America*. Like Ms. Masterson is Veronica Verve and the Rocketeers are the audience, and if I dance well enough, I'll make it to the next episode. Or, I guess, I'll live to see tomorrow because Ms. Masterson won't chop me up and sell my pork chops.

I try out the new move a couple more times to make sure I have it right.

A couple of the dancers clap.

Casey Price does not clap, but she doesn't stop watching. She's watching me dance like I'm the only other person here.

I do my new move one more time, slowly so everyone can see how it works.

> *See? It's not even that hard . . . just a little extra boo-yah to—*

[whistle whistle whistle]

Before anyone can try it, Ms. Masterson flings an arm out in a very not-dancy way and points behind her.

> *EVERYONE BACK TO PRACTICE!*

She flings her mad finger at me now.

> *AND YOU!*

I jump up in one smooth move with my palms up like I am a Wild West bank teller and Ms. Masterson is a Wild West cowboy who just yelled, STICK 'EM UP!

GET OUT OF HERE BEFORE I CALL SOMEONE TO GET *YOU OUT OF HERE.*

I start to back away and a couple dancers clap, as if this were all a super-weird planned routine or something.

I hear someone say,

Maybe he has a point.

Casey Price looks over her shoulder, maybe at the person who said I was right, then she looks straight at me and slow-claps, like Mae Michaelson does on *Fierce Across America* when someone surprises her with *the amount of heart they put into that routine.*

I do a quick worm with my arms as a way to say thank you for the slow-clapping, then I run away as fast as I can before Ms. Masterson calls someone to get me out of here.

I yell over my shoulder:

You're welcome for that super-sweet dance move!
Let me know when you need some more!

Ms. Masterson blows her whistle at me and shoos her hand in my direction. Behind her, Casey Price worms her arms at me until another dancer grabs her and drags her back off toward the gym.

I run all the way to the 315 bus stop and when I get there, I'm huffing and puffing so hard that my heartbeats fill my ears with cotton. No one else is here, so I lay down on the bench to catch my breath and I smile at the sky.

That could have gone a lot worse.

ACTUAL PRELIMS

JORDAN J'S TO-DO LIST OF THINGS TO DO BEFORE FAM PRELIMS, WHICH ARE TODAY OMG HOW IS TODAY TODAY ALREADY

1. check in with Mo even if it isn't real Mo, and is just MindMo
    - **a.** MindMo. Ha! I just made that up!
2. deep cleansing breaths at least a lot of times so I don't explode
3. figure out where that beeping noise is coming from
    - **a.** found it!
        - **i.** it was my phone
            - **1.** Javi wants me to meet him in Sandbox to help with some fairy thing
                - **a.** I never thought I'd say this, but I don't really have time for Sandbox right now
                    - **i.** now Ben Y is texting me to help
                        - **1.** ok, fine
                            - **a.** there's ALWAYS time for Sandbox
                                - **i.** duh, Self

Dear Mind Mo,

Tomorrow is finally the day for <u>Fierce Across America</u> tryouts!

A week ago I didn't even know about them!

And in a whole week I created my own dance!

And I created some totally new dance moves!

Mo.

Seriously.

Mo.

Listen.

I have a concern.

That's why I'm writing you a letter instead of making a list.

A letter seemed better.

Okay, so:

14% of my concern is that Mom won't be able to get a ticket even though tickets are first-come-first-serve-free and parents get tickets no matter what.

23% of my concern is that I will dance my best dancing and my best dancing will still only be clown music–level dancing.

39% of my concern is that I'm afraid I will try to hug Veronica Verve and security will escort me out like they did to that guy last season and I'll miss my shot like he did.

43% of my concern is that I might have a heart attack onstage tomorrow.

⟶

79% of my concern is that I might feel every feeling all at once and all those feelings will make me possibly literally explode onstage and/or cry really hard like I did when Mom and Dad said the trial period of puppy testing was over and Ben Hur was officially a good fit for our family and we could adopt her for real.

Do you remember that, Mo?
I cried for a bunch of days?

Because I was so happy?

But maybe also because I still missed Spartacus, who was the BEST fit for our family and still is even though she's a ghost dog now?

And I didn't even KNOW that's why I was crying.

But you knew, Mo.

You know a lot of things, even though sometimes I don't want to admit that.

And just so you know, the only reason I don't like admitting it is because you get very . . . MO . . . when you hear me say those words.

I already know that when you read this letter you're going to get to this part and you're going to look at me over the top of your glasses and you're going to say:

Can you say more about what getting very MO means to you?

Sure.
Fine.
When you get very . . . MO . . . about something it means you get this happy little crease between your eyes.

That happy little crease feels like it's hiding the words I told you so.

I don't love to be told so, Mo.

Anyway, I ALSO don't want to possibly literally explode from feelings on the FAM stage.
Or really ever.
But especially in front of Veronica Verve.

I know it will be too late to talk to you about all of this when I see you in person, but it has weirdly made me feel better just to write it all out and imagine what you might say to me.

Was that part of your plan all along, Mo?

See! I told you you're smarter than you look.

Haha.

Just kidding.

⟶

You look very smart, especially when you wear two pairs of glasses.

OK, well, I am 95% starving right now so I'm going to go.

Bye, Mo.
I'll talk to you irl soon, I hope.

Peace out,
Jordan J

PS:
How are you doing?
I know that you say our sessions are not about how YOU are doing, but still.
I hope I didn't hurt your feelings when I talked about your I told you so crease.
I didn't mean it in a mean way.

PPS:
I know you know I didn't mean it in a mean way.

PPPS:
Because you know everything.

PPPPS:
I bet you've got the I told you so crease right now.

PPPPPS:
I told you so! Haha.

< Not Newspaper Typing Club Chat >

JORDANJMAGEDDON!!!! ENTERS CHAT

JORDANJMAGEDDON!!!!: Sorry I don't really have much time to help with the fairy fortress farm or whatever it is now, beca

CHAT INFRACTION

JORDANJMAGEDDON!!!!: Javier texted me and said you y'alls needed my help really quick.

JORDANJMAGEDDON!!!!: Wait.

JORDANJMAGEDDON!!!!: What is that???!!!!

JORDANJMAGEDDON!!!!: Is that ME in the sky?

JORDANJMAGEDDON!!!!: Am I made of sparkling fairies???

BenBee: Ben Y coated them with a sparkle potion.

0BenwhY: Just to make them pop a little, without actually making them pop.

BenBee: Then we chained them together in a Jordan J shape.

0BenwhY: humanely, of course.

jajajavier:): We made the chains out of flowers.

JORDANJMAGEDDON!!!!: Because I love flowers????

jajajavier:): Totallllllly.

0BenwhY: And also because fairies love to eat flowers.

JORDANJMAGEDDON!!!!: Look at them all up there! I can tell they're in a me shape because of the hair swoop!

BenBee: That was Javi's idea.
BenBee: Then we shot them into the sky with a cannon, boom.

jajajavier:): I did that part, too.

JORDANJMAGEDDON!!!!: YOU Y'ALLS!!! I love it so much!!!

jajajavier:): We know how much the FAM tryouts mean to you, Jordan.

0BenwhY: And you really are the best dancer I've ever met.

BenBee: We just wanted to wish you luck.

0BenwhY: And since you've made me watch a billion FAM episodes with you,
0BenwhY: I've learned one very important thing . . .

JORDANJMAGEDDON!!!!: Always point your toes if you're dancing traditional ballet??

0BenwhY: Um, yes? And ALSO dancers say break a leg, not good luck.

0BenwhY: So . . .

0BenwhY: OK, Javi, GO!

jajajavier:): Break a leg tomorrow, Jordan!

0BenwhY: Break a leg, dingleberry.

BenBee: Break a leg!

JORDANJMAGEDDON!!!!: Whoaaaaaaaaa.

JORDANJMAGEDDON!!!!: Cooooooooool.

JORDANJMAGEDDON!!!!: Javi!

JORDANJMAGEDDON!!!!: How did you do that?

jajajavier:): Cannon + de-sparkling potion + amazing aim = one sky Jordan with a broken leg.

0BenwhY: No fairies were harmed in the making of this sky Jordan injury.

jajajavier:): yeah, they're still up there, but without their sparkles they blend into the night sky.

jajajavier:): If you turn up your volume you can just barely hear them cursing my name.

JORDANJMAGEDDON!!!!: ty ty ty ty ty ty for breaking my fairy sky leg, you y'alls.

BenBee: Are you nervous for tomorrow?

0BenwhY: Why would you ask that???

BenBee: Why not?

0BenwhY: Of course he's nervous!

JORDANJMAGEDDON!!!!: I mean, kind of, but not really?
JORDANJMAGEDDON!!!!: As long as I don't freak out
JORDANJMAGEDDON!!!!: or have a heart attack
JORDANJMAGEDDON!!!!: or start excited-crying onstage
JORDANJMAGEDDON!!!!: or try to hug Veronica Verve and get hauled out by security
JORDANJMAGEDDON!!!!: I'll be fine?
JORDANJMAGEDDON!!!!: I've practiced all I can practice.
JORDANJMAGEDDON!!!!: I've even practiced taking lots of deep cleansing breaths even though taking lots of deep breaths ma

CHAT INFRACTION

0BenwhY: Don't forget to keep us posted!

BenBee: Break all your legs tomorrow, Jordan.

jajajavier:): you can break mine, too, for extra luck.

JORDANJMAGEDDON!!!!: kk you y'alls.

JORDANJMAGEDDON!!!!: ty again!

JORDANJMAGEDDON!!!! HAS EXITED CHAT

jajajavier:): Can you imagine seeing him on TV every week?

PlanetSafeAce: You mean on FAA?

jajajavier:): No, I mean on FAM, Fierce Across Ame—Ohhhhhh.

BenBee:

BenBee: Wait.

BenBee: Are we the only people in the world who call it FAM?

0BenwhY: We learned about it from Jordan, so . . . yeah, probably.

jajajavier:): Well I'm not going to tell Jordan he's wrong. Are you?

0BenwhY: No way! He wouldn't believe me anyway.

jajajavier:): ja ja ja ja!

BenBee: They should change the name just so he'll be right.

0BenwhY: Fierce Across . . . uh . . .

BenBee: 🤔

PlanetSafeAce: 🤔

BenBee: think he'll make it to callbacks?

jajajavier:): If anyone can do it, Jordan can do it.

0BenwhY: And you know . . .
0BenwhY: even if he doesn't make callbacks at first?
0BenwhY: he can probably talk his way into a spot.

jajajavier:): ja ja ja ja 😂

BenBee: 💯
BenBee: Now. Who wants to help me get those fairies back down to the farm?

jajajavier:):

jajajavier:): I didn't think about that part.

jajajavier:): Fairies hold a grudge, you know.

0BenwhY: I know! That's why I used flowers to link them all together!

0BenwhY: I was VERY gentle! And they can EAT the flowers!

BenBee: Do they *know* they can eat-escape?

PlanetSafeAce: Eatscape!

0BenwhY: I think yes? But they haven't yet because they're coordinating their revenge?

jajajavier:): Uh. I think my mom needs me for something.

jajajavier:) HAS EXITED CHAT

0BenwhY: Yeah, wow, it's late and I have a lot of homework.

BenBee: You never do your homework!

0BenwhY HAS EXITED CHAT

PlanetSafeAce: I also need to eatscape from this chat.

PlanetSafeAce HAS EXITED CHAT

JJ11347 ENTERS CHAT

JJ11347: Hey, you y'alls, sorry I'm late.

JJ11347: Thank you for inviting me into your hallowed non-school server.

JJ11347: I promise not to stay long.

JJ11347: Hang on . . .

JJ11347: Where did everyone go?

JJ11347: Did I miss it?

JJ11347: Darn! 🥺

BenBee: Hi Ms. J.

JJ11347: Hi, Ben B.

JJ11347: I apologize for being late.

JJ11347: Are those very angry fairies in the sky?

BenBee: Yes.

JJ11347: Are they in the shape of a . . . Jordan?

BenBee: Yes.

JJ11347: Creative!

BenBee: Thanks.

BenBee: Uh, Ms. J?

JJ11347: Yes?

BenBee: We saved you a job, since you missed setup.

JJ11347: Oh, did you?

BenBee: Yes?

BenBee: We assigned you fairy cleanup duty.

JJ11347: I see.

BenBee: Good luck.

BenBee: I mean break a leg.

BenBee: Should be easy enough.

BenBee: All you have to do is explain to them that they can eat their way out.

JJ11347: Eat their way out?

BenBee: of the flower vines 0BenwhY tied them up with.

JJ11347: "of the flower vines *with which* 0BenwhY tied them."

BenBee: You don't have to talk fancy, Ms. J. Just tell it to them straight.

BenBee: And you might want to put on some armor.

BenBee: Welcome to the Divergent Dingleberries Non-School Server!

BenBee: Bye!

BenBee HAS EXITED CHAT

JJ11347: Fairy cleanup duty???

JJ11347: This is the last Sandbox party I'm ever late to.

FIERCE ACROSS AMERICA

Season 15

IMPORTANT PRELIMINARY AUDITION INFORMATION

Welcome, Dancers,

We are fiercely excited to welcome you to our CENTRAL FLORIDA auditions! Please read these instructions carefully. Failure to follow instructions may result in disqualification.

1) Upon arrival, please get in line and wait patiently.
2) The line closes at 11 a.m.
3) Anyone who arrives AFTER 11 a.m. will not be allowed in line.
4) You will be given a number. Please DO NOT get out of line to seek out your number.
5) Patience is queen.
6) Fill out all paperwork PRIOR to your number being called.
7) If you are under eighteen, you MUST have a parent or guardian sign your paperwork.
8) If you are under sixteen, you MUST have a parent or guardian sign your paperwork AND be present when you audition.

9) No audition may be longer than TWO minutes.

10) No audition may include more than ONE dancer.

11) Dancers will be called to the stage in groups of FOUR.

12) You may leave the stage AFTER your tryout is complete.

13) If you are NOT onstage when your number is called, you will have TWO MINUTES to appear onstage. Otherwise, you WILL BE disqualified.

14) Callback lists will be posted after EVERYONE has auditioned, though the judges reserve the right to make immediate decisions as they see fit.

15) Do not speak to the judges unless they ask you a question.

16) Do not approach the judges.

17) Do not touch the judges.

18) Anyone acting in an offensive or unprofessional manner will be removed from line, or from the stage, based on the discretion of security and/or the judges, and WILL BE disqualified.

Thank you for your dedication and cooperation!

FAM PRELIMS!*

I have never seen a line this long in my entire life, and I have been to Food World with Dad on a Sunday.

✓ 2 deep cleansing breaths at least a lot of times so I don't explode

I guess a good thing about standing in line for hours and hours is that you have plenty of time to take deep cleansing breaths and also you get to make friends with other people in line.

Like Rebecca who is standing in front of me.

I have never seen anyone sparkle as much as Rebecca. Her clothes, her hair, her skin, even her voice somehow.

I should have asked Javier to come stand in line with me.
Or Ben Y.
Or Ben B.
Or all of them.

Why didn't I ask anyone to come watch me? I mean, Mom HAD to come because I'm a kid, and she WANTS to watch me because

*Held at the famous Ding Darling Auditorium, which is a hilarious name, but a real person's name so it's not nice to laugh at it even though it's really hard not to.

she's my mom, but what about my actual friends? Even if the first-come-first-serve-free-ticket line was way too long for any of them to get tickets, at least they could *stand* here with me.

I can't believe my only friend here is someone I just met four hours ago! How well do you have to know someone before they cheer for you? What if no one cheers for me??? Why am I only thinking of this NOW??????

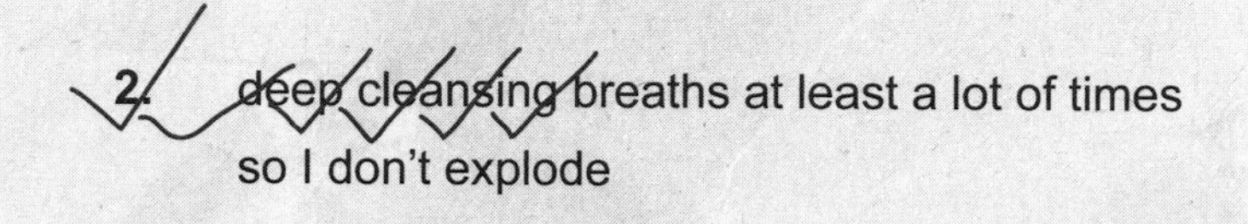

I say to myself in my own brain (instead of saying it to Mom, who is absolutely not leaving, but who has definitely gone to sit in the car because she needs a minute of quiet): *I worry that maybe I should be more sparkly?*

Rebecca turns around, and either I said those words out loud, or she can hear inside my brain. She reaches into her gigantically huge sparkly bag and holds out a shiny bottle of glittery lotion.

> *Want some? You can use it anywhere. Arms, face, wherever you need glitter. It only itches for a minute or two, then you're good.*

Rebecca is not smiling or laughing.

2 deep cleansing breaths at least a lot of times
so I don't explode

I worry we are all going to turn into skeletons
standing in this line.

2 deep cleansing breaths at least a lot of times
so I don't explode

After one hundred thousand million years of standing in line and after not eating the sandwich Mom brought over for me and after deciding that not being sparkly enough is better than being any kind of itchy . . .

after alllllllll of that . . .

omg omg omg

a guy just took my application and he gave me a square of paper with the number 1313 on it and also a safety pin so I can pin it on my shirt and

omg omg omg

Mom and I are finally allowed to walk INSIDE the lobby of the auditorium.

At the exact same time, we both look up at the fancy millionaire dangly lights hanging from the tall tall ceiling.

Also at the exact same time, we both go *ahhhhhh* because the air-conditioning feels sooooooooo good after being out in the sticky hot for so long.

It smells like sweat and feet in here, and there are people everywhere who are practicing intensely bonkers super-sweet dance moves all at the same time, and some people are crying and maybe I might cry too and

omg omg omg

Mom bonks my shoulder with her shoulder and uses her head to point over there so I look over there and whoaaaaa.

Video cameras!

Like, actual TV-show video cameras!

And people with clear earbuds in one ear!

And they're very seriously saying stuff like,

Go to camera two and get a shot of the line.

omg omg omg

Mom finishes signing a permission form and she hands it back to the guy who gave it to her and she laughs and shakes her head a little bit.

If you do well, you might end up being rich and
famous, kiddo.
No more money problems!
Dad and I will be your dependents.

She shakes her head again and smiles, and

omg omg omg

Some lady who has the blackest eyeliner I have ever seen even though I have seen Ben Y's eyeliner tells me to follow her backstage and Mom kisses my head and wishes me luck and squeezes my hand and looks almost as nervous as I feel, which is funny and weird because she doesn't have to dance at all, she just has to watch me.

omg omg omg

I follow the lady backstage and then onto the actual stage along with three other people.

omg omg omg

Break a leg, Rebecca.

My voice croaks like a frog which is a thing I only ever heard a teacher read from a book and not something that I thought could happen in real life.

Rebecca scratches at the glitter on her arm and I hope I don't literally break a leg by slipping on all the piles of sparkles falling off her.

She looks at me and blinks in the bright stage lights and whispers:

Break a leg, uh . . .

I tell her it's okay to be nervous, everyone is nervous, and then I remind her that my name is Jordan. Jordan J.

Rebecca swallows, looks down at me, and whispers,

I think I'm going to throw up, Jordan J.

omg omg omg

I hop back just as I hear my name again. But where is it coming from?

Jordan J!
Over here!
Hey!

I squint through the bright stage lights and see a kid waving at me from one of the areas in the audience that's off to the side and filled with cheering families and dancers who have already danced.

Who *is* that?
Is that Casey *Price*???
THE Casey Price?
The Rocketeer from school???

She shouts,

Break a leg, JJ!

and I don't hear anything after that because

OMG OMG OMG OMG OMG OMG

I SEE VERONICA VERVE
I SEE HER IN ACTUAL REAL LIFE RIGHT THERE IN FRONT OF ME HOW IS THIS REALLY HAPPENING SHE IS AN ACTUAL HUMAN AND SHE IS WAY SHORTER THAN I THOUGHT AND HER HAIR IS SO WHITE AND JAGGEDY

AND THAT IS SO COOL AND SHE POINTS BOO-YAH FINGERS AT ALL OF US ONSTAGE AND THEN SHE WALKS TO THE JUDGES' TABLE THAT IS WAY OUT IN THE BACK OF THE AUDIENCE SEATS AND I GUESS MAE MICHAELSON IS ALREADY THERE BECAUSE SHE STANDS UP AND WAVES AND THE WHOLE CROWD GOES BANANAS BONKERS AND

OMG OMG OMG OMG OMG OMG

The lady with black eyeliner nods at me and gives my shoulder a little tap with her clipboard and says,

Give it all you've got, 1313,

and then she says into a very small walkie-talkie,

1313 is a go,

and then time slows down and I can see little sparkly bits of dust floating in the bright streams of light that slice through the dimming auditorium lights,

and I can hear my heart pounding like it wants to escape my chest and leap off the stage and run out the doors,

and I remember my deep breaths,

and I smell the smell that only comes from auditoriums filled with excited people,

and the only thing I can see is blinding light and blackness,

and then . . .
It's really happening.
My music starts.
Deep breaths.
I close my eyes.
For one hot second I let all the kisses from Mom and all the Jordan-shaped Sandbox fairies buzz around in my heart and then . . .

I let the music fill me up with its rhythms and feelings,
like I'm the only person in the whole world who can really understand what it's trying to say,
like the music itself trusts ME, Jordan J,
to use my super-sweet dance moves
to translate the story it wants the world to know,
like the music and I are dance partners,
but also storyteller partners,
and everything else in the whole universe,
even my own feelings and thoughts,
pauses
so that for two minutes

I am the music
and the music is me
and together we just . . . tell a really awesome story.

The music ends and my body stops moving—both at the exact same time (!!) which is harder to do than you would think even when you practice every day for lots of days.

For a second, the only things I can hear are the whooshes of fast air puffs coming out of my mouth and the *boom-boom-booms* of my heartbeat in my ears.

Mae Michaelson stands up and smiles RIGHT AT ME!

I hope I'm smiling back through my puffing breaths!

Veronica Verve doesn't stand up, but her hand reaches up.

Veronica Verve's hand touches Mae Michaelson's hand while Veronica Verve stares at me like she can see through me and through the wall behind me and through every atom and maybe even back in time, I don't know.

MAE. DID YOU JUST SEE WHAT I SAW?

Veronica Verve keeps looking at me even though she's talking to Mae Michaelson, and two video-camera people run around me on the stage, and there's a noise from the audience that is like a thousand people all saw a car crash at the same time.

Oh no.
I'm not the car crash, am I??

There's a very long pause where no one says anything or moves and I start to wonder if maybe Veronica Verve has paused time with her staring, but then she leans back in her chair and slowly nods at me while she keeps her hand on Mae's arm until Mae sits back down.

THREE THINGS, NUMBER 1313.

Veronica's voice is always very loud on the show, like so loud other people on other TV shows make fun of her, but wow it is so loud in real life I think it might permanently echo in my ears forever.

ONE.
THAT WAS INTENSE.

The crowd claps and cheers and whew, I am not a car crash.

I think maybe my gigantic excited feelings are going to float out of me in embarrassing squeaky laughs or in throw-up, maybe even both, but hopefully not at the same time.

Veronica Verve pauses because she knows we're all waiting to find out if my super-sweet dance moves were so good they hurt her feelings.

TWO.
WHO IS YOUR CHOREOGRAPHER AND WHERE DO YOU TAKE CLASSES?

My eyes fly around the room looking for answers, just like they do when I get called on in class and don't know any of the answers.

Uh, I don't have a choreographer?
I don't take classes anywhere?
I just . . . make up my own super-sweet dance moves?
And then I link them together?

I don't like how quiet my voice sounds.
I also don't like how all my sentences sound like questions.

Veronica Verve closes her eyes and waves her arms in front of her face really fast like she's being attacked by a swarm of mosquitoes.

WHOA WHOA WHOA.
SO WHAT YOU'RE TELLING ME . . .

Mae Michaelson clears her throat and leans so close to her microphone, her mouth might actually be touching it. Gross.

Us.

Mae's voice is very echo-y and loud.

What you're telling US . . .

Some people in the audience laugh but they stop as soon as Veronica Verve stops rolling her eyes at Mae and lasers them back onto me.

SO WHAT YOU'RE TELLING US *IS . . .*
THIS WAS ALL . . .

Veronica Verve swishes her hand up and down at me.

YOU?

I nod.
I don't say anything.
I'm not sure what's happening right now.

WELL THEN . . .
I JUST . . .
HUH . . .

Veronica Verve keeps staring at me, not blinking, and the lights up here onstage are really hot, and even though I love Veronica Verve and I think she's ten-out-of-ten outstanding in every possible way, I wish she could find her words a little bit faster.

I wipe the sweat off my upper lip with the back of my hand.

Veronica Verve starts to nod really slowly.

YOUR DANCE VISION IS . . .
I'VE GOT NO WORDS FOR IT, NUMBER 1313 . . .

Mae Michaelson leans into her microphone again and says loudly,

And trust me.
She absolutely has words for everything.

The audience laughs.

Veronica Verve shoos a hand at Mae, and does not smile or laugh. She leans back in her chair and puts both hands on her head, making triangles out of her arms.

LIKE, PRODIGY-LEVEL I'VE-GOT-NO-WORDS-FOR-IT, KID.
I HAVE HONESTLY NEVER SEEN ANYTHING LIKE THIS.
IN MY ENTIRE DANCING CAREER.

The surprised murmuring noises from the crowd are basically the same noises in my brain, because what does it mean if Veronica Verve says she has no words for my progedy-level dance vision?

What's a progedy?
What even is *dance vision*, exactly?

Does she mean how I create my own moves in my head and with my body?
Has she ever said anything like this to anyone else on the show before?
I'm not sure she has and I've watched every episode a billion trillion times.

Mae Michaelson leans into her microphone and says,

> *Didn't you say you have* three *things to tell this young man?*
> *We do have other dancers waiting to audition, you know.*

Some people in the audience laugh a little bit and I'm starting to feel weird and confused again.

Are they laughing at Mae?
Or at me?

Veronica Verve nods sharply and keeps not smiling and keeps staring at me with her laser eyes.

> *CORRECT.*
> *YES.*
> *THREE THINGS.*
> *ONE: THAT WAS INTENSE.*
> *TWO: IRRELEVENT BECAUSE YOU ARE YOUR*

OWN CHOREOGRAPHER, APPARENTLY.
THREE: UNFORTUNATELY, THIS IS A DANCE COMPETITION, NOT A DANCE-VISION COMPETITION.
YOUR DANCING SKILLS ARE SIX OUT OF TEN, AT BEST, 1313.

I close my eyes so I can repeat her words to myself without being distracted by the bright stage lights or the audience noises.

Wait.
Did she just say SIX out of ten?
At BEST?
What??
No!

THAT MEANS NO CALLBACKS.

I heard *that* with my eyes wide open.

My guts all start melting together in one big steaming waterfall.

Veronica Verve must have found her words because she keeps talking in her super-loud voice and I hear some of it, but mostly I hear the hot waterfall of melting guts crashing around inside me.

HERE'S THE THING, NUMBER 1313 . . .

I squeeze my eyes closed so I can work harder on squeezing my ears closed, but even that doesn't drown out Veronica Verve's loud loud loud loud voice or the hot hot hot lights that make the insides of my eyelids look red and not dark.

I am feeling all the feelings at once and one of those feelings tells me there is some x-treme Jordan-ing about to happen any second.

> *HEY.*
> *NUMBER 1313?*
> *KID?*
> *WHAT'S YOUR NAME?*

I don't want to answer her.
I don't want to be here anymore.

The audience starts to quietly chant *thir-teen, thir-teen, thir-teen.*

I open my eyes, but I don't uncover my ears.
When I talk it sounds like I'm underwater.
I wish I was underwater.

> *Jordan.*

Now the audience is quietly chanting *Jor-dan, Jor-dan, Jor-dan,* or maybe it only seems quiet because I'm still squeezing my ears with my palms.

PLEASE DON'T BE DISAPPOINTED, JORDAN.
I DON'T EVEN HAVE A SCALE TO DESCRIBE
YOUR DANCE VISION.

Veronica Verve sucks in a very loud breath and then breathes out,

PRODIGY-LEVEL CHOREOGRAPHY, KID.
I'VE NEVER SEEN ANYTHING LIKE IT.

Mae Michaelson says,

You've certainly already said *something like that to*
Number 1313, VV.
Repeatedly, in fact, over the past several minutes.
Shall we release him to the wilds now?
Let me answer for you: Yes. Yes we shall.
Thank you, Number 1313.

Go forth and scorch the Earth with your visionary choreo.
We appreciate you.

Mae Michaelson presses her hands together like she's praying and she nods at me and then the backstage lady with the eyeliner appears out of nowhere and pulls me off the stage just as the song for the next dancer starts.

The backstage lady hands me a piece of paper.

No callbacks, 1313.
I hope you're proud of what you did today, though.
Seriously.
I've never seen VV get worked up like that, and I've been with the show all fifteen seasons!

She waves her hand in front of my face.

You okay?

But . . .
No . . .
I . . .
I look up into her black-lined eyes and I try to talk around my crashing melted guts.

The backstage lady pats me on the shoulder and frown-smiles in that way grown-ups do when they look at you and feel bad for you, but still want you to go away.

She gently pushes me out into the big bright hallway and the stage door slams shut behind me, and wait . . .

That's it?
That's all?
It's over?

Hey!
Jordan!

A different kind of loud voice comes up from behind me. Its high pitch bounces around in my ears and does not sound familiar or like it belongs to someone I want to talk to right now, because I want to talk to exactly zero people right now.

With a half smile that pops up in the corner of her mouth just in time to match the way she pops her hip out, Casey Price swings into my line of vision as if she knows how to be everywhere all at once, like a teacher or a mom.

She shakes her long, long, shiny, shiny ponytail, and says with a huge smile,

Killer moves out there, JJ.
Kill-errrrrrr.

I say,

Are you making fun of me?
That would be a very very very rude thing to do right now.

Casey Price raises her eyebrows at me like *I* was just rude to *her*.

WHAT?
NO!
WHAT?

I stare at her like a NOT-rude person who does NOT want to talk about anything to anyone ever again, especially if that thing or that person is related to *Fierce Across America* or dancing or blah.

I sniff and wipe my nose with the back of my hand, which I know is gross, but who cares about anything anymore.

Across the lobby, I notice a Mom-shaped human walking toward me really fast with a really big soda. Yes. Good. Actually Mom.

I try to walk toward her and say bye to Casey Price at the same time.

Okay, well, it was . . . confusing . . . to talk to you, so . . . bye.

Casey Price yells after me:

Hey, JJ?
Maybe you could share your dance vision with me?
Some super-sweet moves for callbacks?

I did NOT just hear Casey Price say she made it to callbacks, I did not just hear that, I did not just hear her ask me to help her with her callbacks routine, I did not hear those words at all.

The only words I hear are: *Six out of ten, at best.*

And: *No callbacks, 1313.*

Casey Price turns around and points at me while she walks away backward, smiling.

She shouts:

Think about it, JJ.

Then I hear Mom yelling, *JORDAN!!!!* and the only thing I can think about is going home and digging a giant hole in the backyard and living in that hole forever.

Mom stops walking toward me for a second because her shout is so excited and so full of feelings that her eyes close and she squats a little bit and wiggles side to side a little bit and spills a little bit of the giant soda she's holding.

YOU WERE SOOOOOOO GOOD!!!!!

And, *what?*

Did she not see me about to launch into some x-treme Jordan-ing in front of the whole everyone?

Did she not hear Veronica Verve say, *Six out of ten, at best*?

Why is Mom still squealing and wiggling and spilling that big drink?

People all around us have stopped walking and talking so they can look at Mom and laugh at her in a nice way, or go *awwwww*, or just smile really big.

One girl walks past and smiles at me and whispers, *Thir-teen, thir-teen, thir-teen.*

I walk really fast over to Mom because it is a little bit embarrassing to have your mom scream your name in public and a LOT embarrassing to have her scream, *You were soooooooo good!!!!!* when everyone around you JUST heard the judges tell you you're *not* actually good at dancing *at all.*

A thought strikes me like a bowling ball dropped out of the sky.

You know when you watch the FAM auditions on TV and they play the clown music for the dancers who are so bad but think they're good? THOSE are the dancers who get sent home early.

Am *I* a clown music dancer?

Mom hands her giant soda to a stranger so she can hug me tight with both arms.

She lets me go after a big squeeze and says thanks to the stranger and takes her soda back and she keeps staring at me like she doesn't even recognize that I am the same Jordan she rode in the car with and stood in line with and tried really hard not to yell at for *never taking a break from talking, not even once, it really is alarmingly impressive, Jordan.*

> *What?*
> *Stop looking at me like that.*

I'm starting to worry that maybe her soda has way too much sugar in it or I don't even know. Mom bounces on her toes, smiling and shaking her head.

> *I know you love the show . . .*
> *And I see how you dance everywhere all the time . . .*
> *And you have that article for the newspaper, which is so cool . . .*
> *And I know you've been practicing in your room for days, but . . .*
> *I didn't think . . .*
> *I didn't know . . .*
> *I just thought . . .*

I guess the theme of the day is grown-ups not having the words to describe me.

Where did you learn to DO that, kiddo?

It's probably time for Mom to bring it down like 6576575 notches because watching her eyeballs get big and excited, and then go back to normal, and then get big and excited again, over and over and over, all while she says things like *Jordan! I'm so impressed!* and *Jordan! You were so good!* and *I just . . . Jordan! WOW! [DEEP BREATH]* She's SO happy and SO loud and SO surprised, it's like I'm watching my own mom figure out IN REAL TIME, IN FRONT OF ME that I'm good at the thing I've always thought *she already thought* I was good at.

I'm used to the Mom Smile asterisks* that mean she wants *me* to believe *she* believes something I did was good or smart or whatever (even though we both know sometimes it's a stretch), but this is a different kind of asterisk than usual.

It's extra sharp, extra asterisk-y.

And it's poking at me over and over, hurting hurting hurting feelings I didn't even know I could have about my own mom.

*Moms always have to be proud of their kids and say nice things because they are moms.

FIERCE ACROSS AMERICA

Season 15

Dear #1313,

Thank you for your participation in *Fierce Across America*'s groundbreaking 15th season.

Without dancers like you, our show would be just another competition show. It's your talent, your spark, and your passion that put the *Fierce* in *Fierce Across America*.

While we are sad to see you go, we encourage you to keep practicing, keep dancing, and make sure to audition again next season.

As a token of our gratitude, please use your personalized coupon code, FAA151313, to get 15% off in our online merch store.

You Are Fiercely Loved,

Mae

Veronica

PLEASE TUNE IN ON WEDNESDAYS THIS SUMMER,
8 P.M. EST/7 P.M. CST, TO WATCH THE YOUNGEST, FIERCEST
COMPETITORS EVER DANCE FOR THEIR LIVES.

Dear Mind Mo,

I know I already wrote you a letter yesterday, but I'm writing another one anyway so I don't ever ever ever ever ever ever ever ever ever have to talk about any of this out loud when I see you again.

I don't even want to talk about it now, actually, so never mind.

Peace out,
Jordan J

A CONVERSATION IN MY MIND WITH MINDMO WHILE MOM DRIVES HOME FROM FAM PRELIMS: NOT REALLY A LIST, BY JORDAN J

My body is tired of feeling feelings, MindMo.

My whole self is tired of it.

I would like a break from feeling feelings.

I don't want to feel anything at all for a while.

I want to float in space.

Away from everything and everyone.

Even away from you.

No offense.

Even away from my ownself.

If we had a bathtub at home I would get in it.

I would float in the dark.
Maybe that would feel like floating in space.

But we don't have a bathtub.

Only a shower.

Which is DUMB.

Who builds a house with no bathtubs????????

The only feelings I'm going to feel right now are feelings about THAT.

I have to go, MindMo, Mom is talking.

MOM'S CAR

I look over at Mom who is looking out at the street because she's driving. I grunt.

Huh?

Mom glances at me really fast, and then looks back out at the road.

Jordan.
Were you not listening to me?
I was just saying that I'm really proud of you.
Don't be so hard on yourself, kiddo.
You were amazing.

Mom reaches over to squeeze the back of my neck in that way I like, but I duck down because I don't want anything to make me feel good right now.

From my ducked-down position, I whip my head around to stare at Mom and all of a sudden that explosion I was afraid might happen onstage starts to happen now, but not in a happy way or an excited way. It's an ugly burst of mad, and I point it right at Mom.

All I want is to disappear!
And forget about this day!
What kind of dumb house doesn't even HAVE A BATHTUB!

Mom doesn't say anything.

She chews her bottom lip.

That always means she's thinking really hard.

She jerks the steering wheel and turns down a street that we almost drove past.

I know this street.

Mom slows the car down and glances at me.

> *Don't use that tone with me ever again.*
> *You hear me?*

I nod.

> *And, yeah.*
> *It IS dumb that we don't have a bathtub.*

I nod again.

> *Get your phone out of my purse.*

I nod one more time, and for a second I wonder if Mom is going to ask me to call a bathtub store. But no.

Call Ben Y and see if it's okay with her mom if you come over for a bath.
Actually . . .
Let me *explain all this to her mom.*
Put it on speaker, will you?

AN ADDENDUM TO THE CONVERSATION IN MY MIND WITH MINDMO WHILE MOM DRIVES ~~HOME~~ TO BEN Y'S HOUSE AFTER FAM PRELIMS: STILL NOT REALLY A LIST, BY JORDAN J

It's Jordan J again, MindMo.

I know you probably figured this out a long time ago,
but I still want to think it out loud to you . . .

My mom is pretty great.

Isn't she?

So is this bathtub.

And I didn't even put any water in it!

BEN Y'S HOUSE / BATHTUB

Hello in there?
Jordan?
Time to return from deep space, okay?
Just in case you don't remember,
we only have one bathroom.
Jordan?
I really have to go!
And that means you REALLY have to go.
Ha ha.
Get it?
Jordan?
I'm coming in.

Ben Y's words bounce around the bathroom before she does, until boom, the door swings open, the light goes on and there she is whipping open the shower curtain and looking down at me.

Feeling any better?

My legs are tingly from being crunched in the empty tub.
My shoes squeak against the porcelain while I wiggle my feet and stretch out my knees.
I guess you really need water in a bathtub to float in it.
I mean, duh.

But I didn't want to take off all my clothes in someone else's bathroom.

I shrug and stand up, blinking in the bright light.

I climb out of the tub and put both hands up on Ben Y's shoulders.

I look straight into her face and try to use my eyes to suck some of the calm awesomeness out of her eyes so I can borrow it for a little while.

Ben Y wiggles out of my grip and half-frowns.

Stop trying to vampire my awesomeness.

I keep staring. No blinking. Only absorbing calm awesomeness.

But I need it.

Ben Y puts her hands on my shoulders and stares back at me.

No you don't.
You have your own awesomeness.

I give her a little push, but I don't let go and I don't stop staring.

Not anymore.

Ben Y pushes back and wobbles my head.

Oh, come on.

Ben Y's mom's head peers around the bathroom door and I like how little wispy bits of hair circle her face instead of neatly fitting in her ponytail.

Mijo—

She smiles at me in the same way you smile at something you think is interesting but don't really understand, like a waterfall made of chickens.

Mijo, it's time to go.
Your mom will be back in five minutes, okay?

I don't feel okay even though I say,

Okay.

Ben Y gives me a quick hug before pushing me out of the bathroom.

I hope my bathtub helped, Jordan.
Sorry it wasn't cleaner.
I also hope you feel better soon.

I make a hopeful fart noise.

Thank you, Ben Y.
And I also am glad about your tub and I also hope I feel better, too.
See you tomorrow.

Ben Y's mom's arm wraps around my shoulder and she squeezes me before she lets go and says,

Congratulations, Mijo. I'm so proud of you.

I look up at her and watch her wispy hairs dance around her ears.

Congratulations, why?! For what?!

I take a deep cleansing breath so that I can take a nicer, quieter tone.

I was one of those dancers they send home early, just like the ones on the show that everyone laughs at because the producers play clown music while they dance which is actually really mean now that I think of it and also now that I might be one of those dancers.

I swallow hard to try and push the choking lump out of my throat.

Veronica Verve hurt MY feelings.
For real.
Not in a compliment-y way at ALL.

Ben Y's mom squeezes me one more time in a kind of half hug and says,

Breathe, Mijo.
Your mom said the judge told you she'd never seen such vision before.
Not from a young person, not from anyone.
Isn't that something to be proud of?
Something worth congratulations?
That sounds like a big thing.

I can feel my mouth pinching shut in a grouchy frown and I don't even try to stop it.

But I use my dance vision to DANCE.
How can one thing be so good while the other one is only six out of ten, at best?
It doesn't make any sense!

The doorbell rings at the same time Ben Y's mom offers up a half smile that looks exactly like Ben Y's half smile. She pats me on the back in a quiet soft way that feels exactly the opposite of all the racing mad thoughts in my body.

I stand by my congratulations.

Ben Y yells through the closed bathroom door:

BYE, JORDAN!

I wave at the closed bathroom door without saying anything because I don't want to say anything and I know Ben Y can't see me but I bet she still knows I'm waving because Ben Y knows me better than I know me sometimes.

Ben Y's mom opens the door and she and Mom say a lot of things with their eyes that they don't say with words and then Mom grabs my hand and pulls me into a hug and we get in the car to go home.

You know why I can't ever figure out what day it is?

Because every day is like fifty days in one.

MOM'S CAR

My sigh comes from every space inside my lungs; one long exhale that keeps going and going and going and going until it feels like my ribs might cave in on each other like a sinkhole over an empty cavern. My body automatically sucks in some too-many-people-in-this-car air before I breathe out again.

I thought just Mom *was coming to get me.*

Dad glances out the window at the passenger-side mirror and I can see him seeing me seeing him seeing me.

Jeez.
Do I have cooties or something?

Carolina laughs and kicks the back of Dad's seat.

Yes!

Mom looks up at the rearview mirror. She blinks from the road to me to the road to me.

We thought maybe we'd all grab some dinner.
You hungry?

I shake my head but maybe she can't see it because her eyes are not looking in the rearview mirror. Dad twists around so he can actually look at me.

You sure?
We could grab a cheeseburger at Fran's.
Double-chocolate milkshake?

A Fran's double-chocolate milkshake is usually the cure for everything, including after you have to get a shot, or after you get your report card, or when you find out you have to go to summer school, or pretty much anything. Well, except for a stomachache. Fran's double-chocolate milkshakes only *cause* stomachaches, but that's okay because a Fran's stomachache is totally worth it any day.

The problem right now is that I one hundred percent know that Mom and Dad do not have enough money to be buying five-dollar milkshakes, because yesterday Mom yelled at Dad, *What?! You went to Fran's?! ROCK! We can't afford five-dollar milkshakes right now!!* And then Dad said, *But we can't afford* not *to treat ourselves when we get good news, right?* And Mom said, *What good news?* And Dad smiled his evil-villain smile and said, *The good news is . . . today is not yesterday, and any day that isn't yesterday is worth celebrating.* Then Mom rolled her eyes and laughed and stole his milkshake and said, *No more five-dollar milkshakes,* while she sucked hard on the straw and smiled her own evil-villain smile.

I can't seem to stop sighing.

It's like I have too much air in me to feel as deflated and wilty as I need to feel.

I have to talk and sigh at the same time.

I thought we didn't have any money for five-dollar milkshakes.
Everyone's always talking about no money no money no money.
There's no money for the art supplies I need.
There's no money to bring anything that's not a wrinkly hot dog in my lunch every day.
There's no money to see Mo like I used to—

Carolina interrupts with a laugh and says,

Maybe Mo should pay US for giving her a vacation from YOU!

Out of nowhere, big loud angry words fly out of my mouth.

Shut UP, Carolina!
No one asked you!
No one ever asks you, because you're only nine and all you ever do is say dumb things! AND you eat all the good donuts ON PURPOSE when you KNOW there isn't enough money to buy MORE donuts!

Carolina shrieks,

I DO NOT!

She lunges at me and I curl up in the Pork Chop Protection Ball™.

Dad twists around again and says,

Whoaaaaaaaaaa.
Jordan, my dude.
Not okay.
Carolina, my Carolina.
You need to learn to read the room.

Mom hits the brakes and pulls the car over into a gas station so she can turn around and look at us with both of her eyes.

My nose is dripping and I sniff big and loud and look at my lap and wish I was back in Ben Y's bathtub trying not to feel any feelings.

Mom and Dad both take off their seat belts at the same time and get out of the car and I think maybe they're going inside the gas station to get away from me and Carolina.

Instead, it's an ambush.

Both doors to the back seat open, Mom on my side and Dad on Carolina's.

Scooch.
Scooch.

I unbuckle my seat belt and scooch and Mom squishes me into the middle seat and Carolina unbuckles her seat belt and scooches and Dad squishes her into *me*, and now Carolina and I are the ham and cheese in a back-seat family sandwich.

Jordan.
Look at me.

Mom puts her hand under my chin and very gently lifts my face so that I can see her face. She grabs me in a sneak-attack hug and smushes my face into her shoulder and says,

Aw, bud.
I'm really, really sorry.
I know how disappointed you are.
But you can't talk to your sister like that, okay?

I sniff and nod into Mom's shoulder and I know that she knows I already feel bad for yelling at Carolina like that. I can't help it. I don't like it when anyone yells, even my ownself.

Mom lets go of me and pushes some hair off my forehead even though it wasn't in my eyes.

And listen, it isn't your job to worry about money.
Okay?
One billion trillion percent not your job.
That's my job.

Now Dad grabs me in a sneak-attack hug except his has Carolina smushed in it, too. Over Carolina's muffled giggles, he says,

And my job.

I nod a little bit because I really don't want it to be my job.

Your job,

Mom says, pulling me out of Dad's hug and gently bonking foreheads with me while she looks down into my eyes,

is to enjoy a milkshake without any worries.

That makes me laugh a little bit.

Your job,

she says, bonking me again,

is to be a kid and do kid things and make mistakes and learn lessons.

Dad twists around and leans his forehead into my forehead and Mom's forehead, and somehow Carolina is under all of us now, and we really need to get a bigger car one day, when there's more money.

Carolina peers up into all our faces and says she would like her job to be eating donuts.

Mom pushes back from all of us and looks at me for a long time before she says,

My job—and Dad's job—is to support you, and encourage you, and keep you alive while you learn those lessons.

Dad leans back into the seat, though his head is turned to look at us. He tosses his long arm around my shoulders AND Mom's shoulders. I can feel his muscles tense up as he squeezes Mom. Her voice is wobbly now as she whispers,

It's also our job to make sure you two know that we are the grown-ups and you are the kids. Never vice versa.

I nod.

Carolina nods.

I can tell Dad is thinking about making a joke, but he reads the room and just nods instead.

Mom leans back on Dad's arm and sighs out her own long, long, long sigh, then she snakes her arm up, still under his, but so her hand rests on the back of my neck in the way that I like because it feels kind of heavy and warm.

I take a deep breath and maybe I breathe in some of her long sigh-y sigh, and maybe it will make me feel better to have a little bit of Mom's breath filling up my sad and tired lungs.

We are all tangled up in one big back-seat family sandwich ball and no one says anything for a little bit even though it's starting to get really hot and stuffy and Carolina's breath smells like hot dogs.

Mom's voice is deep and quiet in just the way that I like when she says,

So.

Dad's voice is even deeper, and always jokey-sounding, even if he doesn't mean to be jokey.

So?

They both say,

Fran's?

at the same time, as if they planned it.

Carolina nods, but I shake my head. Leaning on Mom's warm arm has made all the tired rise up into my brain until it must weigh a million pounds.

Home it is, my sweet prodigy.
Rain check, my sweet Carolina.

Mom and Dad climb out of the back seat, get back in the front seat, click their seat belts, wait to hear our seat belts click, and then zoom . . . off we go into the dark night.

Carolina must be really tired, too, because she doesn't even complain about the double-chocolate rain check.

I want to ask Mom what *progedy* means, but my tired won't let my voice interrupt the sleepy, quiet driving noises.

I'm starting to guess it might not be terrible, even though I don't know how it can be good if it also means I'm a bad dancer.

THINGS TO THINK ABOUT INSTEAD OF THINKING ABOUT THE THING THAT RHYMES WITH SHMALL-BACKS: A LIST BY JORDAN J

1. literally everything else in the whole world except for that 1 thing

< Newspaper Typing Club Chat >

jajajavier:): Dude, that's how parents ARE. How are you just now realizing this?
jajajavier:): They're always thinking something weird about you or not telling you something . . .
jajajavier:): Or acting surprised when you do something they don't expect.

JORDANJMAGEDDON!!!!: or ambushing you into a family sandwich in the back seat of the car when all you want is to be by yo

CHAT INFRACTION

jajajavier:): Isn't the important thing that you made them proud?

JORDANJMAGEDDON!!!!: Is surprised the same as proud, tho? 🤷

BenBee ENTERS CHAT

BenBee: How did it go??? How did it go??? How did it go???
BenBee: I tried to set the recorder for the audition episodes of FAM's next season, but it's too far away so

CHAT INFRACTION

BenBee: IS THAT MY FIRST EVER CHAT INFRACTION?

BenBee: SOMEONE FIND ALL THE LOGS!

jajajavier:): Literally no one is going to do that, Ben B. 😄 😵

jajajavier:): But 🏆 congrats on your possibly first ever chat infraction.

jajajavier:): May there be more in your future.

0BenwhY ENTERS CHAT

0BenwhY: Heyo. You okay, J-dawg?

PlanetSafeAce ENTERS CHAT

PlanetSafeAce: ???

CHAT INFRACTION

jajajavier:): I second Ace.

jajajavier:): Spill, Jordan.

jajajavier:): WHAT HAPPENED?

jajajavier:): Other than me texting you 1285762140756 times and you not answering.

jajajavier:): And now finding out that your mom was super excited that you were awesome . . .

jajajavier:): but you don't like that for some weird reason . . .

0BenwhY: But he IS awesome.

0BenwhY: You ARE, Jordan.

0BenwhY: I can see you looking at me over your monitor!

0BenwhY: idc if we aren't allowed to talk while we play Sandbox in the library, I might still come over there

CHAT INFRACTION

0BenwhY: and yell in your face

0BenwhY: because you ARE awesome and you should believe that.

0BenwhY: Also, you ARE weird!

jajajavier:): And that's why we love you.

0BenwhY: Exactly.

PlanetSafeAce: Yeahhhhhh. Come on, Jordan. We need the hot dance deets, yo!

0BenwhY: No. Ace. Never say hot dance deets ever again.

PlanetSafeAce: Give us the hXX dXXXX dXXXs Jordan!

JORDANJMAGEDDON!!!!: CHAT INFRACTION.

BenBee: Uh.

JORDANJMAGEDDON!!!!: CHAT INFRACTION.

0BenwhY: What are you doing? You can't just TYPE chat infraction.

JORDANJMAGEDDON!!!!: CHAT INFRACTION!

JORDANJMAGEDDON!!!!: Jordan has been ejected from dancing! 😖 😫

JORDANJMAGEDDON!!!!: He's going to live in a hole in his backyard! 😖 😫

JORDANJMAGEDDON!!!!: And never talk about any of this again! 😖 😫

JORDANJMAGEDDON!!!! HAS EXITED CHAT

JJ11347 ENTERS CHAT

JJ11347: I hate to interrupt . . .

JJ11347: But! The morning announcements are about to begin and I need everyone to be logged off and ready to

CHAT INFRACTION

BenBee: 

0BenwhY: akshgflkhsa

jajajavier:): ja ja ja!

PlanetSafeAce:

SCHOOL*

Let's START the day with KUDOS, shall WE?

When Mr. Mann does the morning announcements, or any kind of announcement, or really any kind of talking, he always seems to not know where the exclamation points should go.

> *KUDOS to Rocketeer Casey Price for making it to callbacks DURING this past weekend's America Is FIERCE television competition. FURTHER kudos to seventh GRADER Jordan Johnson for auditioning as WELL.*

Ben Y's eyeballs are huge as she points to the speaker on the ceiling.

Ben B's mouth somehow hangs open and smiles at the same time.

Javier nods and smiles.

*Before school, in the library, because this is where we all hang out now that Ms. J is our librarian instead of our teacher, and because the library is a lot bigger than room 113 under the stairs,** which is where we used to play Sandbox on computers Ms. J borrowed after we convinced her to play Sandbox with us in return for reading out loud.

**Oh, *that's* why she calls us her kids under the stairs! Aha!

Mr. Mann's voice still echoes down from the ceiling speaker:

> *It's always nice to see Hart Rockets ROCKETING to fame and FORTUNE!*
> *Speaking of fame, today's lunch includes the famously delicious SALISBURY steak and corn and—*

Wait . . . was that *me* Jordan?
Who just got kudo'd by Mr. Mann?
It had to be, right?
How many other dancing Jordans could possibly go to this school?

I've never been kudo'd on the announcements before! That's for smart kids and kids who win things, except I didn't win anything and I'm smart in my own *divergent* way—which Ms. J says doesn't mean dumb, but I've never gotten the idea that anyone else thinks it means *smart.*

Also, Mr. Mann got my name wrong. But still, he must have meant me, right? I guess I can try out being Jordan *Johnson* for a minute or two and see how that feels.

Everyone is talking at once now, drowning out Mr. Mann who is still talking about lunch, and I am having three thoughts at the same time:

1) How did Mr. Mann even know I was *at* FAM tryouts?

2) It bothers me more that Mr. Mann got the name of the show wrong than it does that he got MY name wrong. Is that weird?

3) I forgot the third thought.

Ms. J appears at my side so fast it's like she literally flew over as a bird or a bat or some kind of fast bug and then BAM turned into her regular self.

Kudos, Jordan JACKSON, no relation.

And the way Ms. J smiles at me like she knows a secret makes me wonder if maybe she's the one who told Mr. Mann about me auditioning.

Everyone is saying *congratulations* and *kudos*—even kids I don't know—which is a little confusing because I'm a *six out of ten, at best* dancer who tried his best and who's probably going to get rudely clown music'd when Season 15 premieres, and who didn't even get to callbacks.

That feels very definitely like an embarrassing thing, not a congratulations thing, so why am I the only person who's confused right now?

When the bell rings, a bunch of kids from the dance team appear out of nowhere and walk out of the library with me and their questions stumble over each other, overlapping and building in volume, and most of them want to know what Veronica Verve is like in real life and my confused feelings start to get replaced with a bubbly excited feeling because I can actually, mostly answer their questions.

The bubbly excited feeling makes my feet bounce when I walk, and bouncing feet make me want to *hype a leap*, which is something I heard a kid say when he was practicing at prelims.

I hype a leap and then another one, and you know what? If I hype a leap near a wall, I can leap and then fling out a foot to the side to push off the wall and extend the leap into a spin before I land.

I'm going to call that a HYPER leap.

Sweet.

I test out my new hyper leap right there in the hallway on the way to first period and a couple of kids clap and I might just spin all the way through the ceiling and into the sky like a sky Jordan made of myself instead of angry fairies.

Get it, JJ!
Hype that leap!

I whip my head around, midair, because I recognize that voice, and yep.

Casey Price's very sparkly brown eyes watch me wave bye to Javi and keep watching as I leap over to her.

Nice neck pop, too.
That on purpose?
Or no?

Her very, very black and shiny long hair is twisted into a ponytail that falls over one shoulder. I wonder if it ever gets caught in her backpack straps. That would hurt, I bet.

My brain knows that I shouldn't be mad at Casey Price for making it to callbacks, even though some other part of me is definitely kind of mad at her.

Or maybe I'm jealous and my jealous is still defining its identity? I don't know. I should write that down and ask Mo about it.

I try not to sound mad when I say,

It's called a hyper leap, *Casey Price, and yes, the neck pop is on purpose.*
Why even bother spinning if you aren't going to add some pop to your spot?

Casey Price laughs her hot-pink laugh and it's so high-pitched my eyes water a little bit.

> *Touché, my friend.*
> *Touché.*

Neither one of us says anything for a second while I try to sort out why Casey Price just called me her friend, and then all in one big rush she says,

> *I know you're probably upset about not making it to—*

I hold up my hand and shout:

> *CHAT INFRACTION!*

Casey Price's mouth is still open, mid-word, and she takes a very tiny step back as if my words knocked her off-balance for a second. She closes her mouth in a line that's almost a smile and she points her eyebrows into a *V* and tilts her head at me.

Seriously, she isn't even dancing—she's barely even moving—and it still somehow looks like she's dancing. How does she DO that?

She holds up *her* hand now.

Have you thought about what I proposed?
At all?
What do you think about working together?
For the . . . uh . . .
Competition That Shall Not Be Named?

I'm not sure how to answer her because I'm not exactly sure what she's asking, other than probably a thing I definitely do not want to do.

The *You-Better-Hope-You-Don't-Have-a-Teacher-Who-Locks-the-Classroom-Door-After-the-Bell-Rings* bell rings.

Casey Price glances down the hall as kids scatter.
She looks back at me.

Meet me after school?
By the big tree with the drooping branches?
We can talk more about it?
I need your prodigy-level dance vision, JJ.

I still don't say anything because I still don't know what to say.

Casey Price points at me just like she did at prelims, starts walking away backward, smiles, and says:

What if I pay you?

Pay me?
For my progedy-level dance vision, whatever that means?
Hmm.
I wonder if she'd pay me enough to buy my own art supplies.

My face must do something because Casey Price, who is still walking backward and watching me, laughs that hot-pink laugh again and jabs the air with her still-pointing finger.

That's what I thought.

She flings herself around to walk forward and her shiny ponytail whips back and forth in a hyper leap of its own.

PROS AND CONS OF SHARING MY DANCE VISION WITH CASEY PRICE: A PRO AND CON LIST BY JORDAN J

1. what if my dance moves aren't good enough
2. what if my dance moves ARE good enough and Casey Price takes all the credit for them
3. what if I don't actually like her very much
4. what if she doesn't actually like ME very much
5. do you have to like each other to work together?
6. maybe not, but that wouldn't be very fun and I would be sad if dancing wasn't fun anymore
7. I would also be sad if teaching someone my dance moves wasn't fun because it seems like it would be really fun
8. is this a pro/con list?
9. I don't think it is
10. money

AFTER SCHOOL AT THE TREE WITH DROOPING BRANCHES

Casey Price stands under the tree that Ms. J used for forest-bathing during summer school when Ben B and Ben Y and Javier and I all made her feel her feelings and then she yelled at us and then she said she was sorry and then we convinced her to play Sandbox with us and she convinced us to read books with her.

A bunch of kids run past me to the buses or their parents' cars or just away, away, away.

The tree's branches swish in the hot breeze as Casey Price waves at me, swishing her hand through the hot breeze.

> *There he is!*
> *Mr. Veronica Verve Jr.!*
> *JJ, J!*

She makes *rahhhhhh* crowd noises in her cupped hands as I walk up.

Sometimes it's hard for me to figure out if people are making fun of me or joking about me, or if they're actually saying things they really mean. Sometimes I think it's all three at once. Sometimes I *know* it's all three at once. Almost all the time I don't really care because just like Mo says, *You have enough going on in your brain, Jordan, don't let anyone take up space in there unless you want them to.*

But the thing is, Casey Price already lives in my brain a little bit even though I only know how good she is at dancing and not how good she is at being a nice person. I would rather not know the real Casey Price if the real Casey Price is someone who makes fun of me or jokes about me or says things that are mean, but the kind of tricky mean I can't figure out until someone else laughs.

Casey Price rests a palm on her popped hip and taps her fingers while she stares at me staring at her.

I stare back, but I also stare a little bit over her shoulder and past the tree to see if Ben Y is already on her way to catch the 315.

Casey Price drops into a perfect split that's so smooth and fast and surprising, it's my turn to take a tiny but surprised step backward. She looks up at me, and says,

> *Here's my idea.*
> *And my offer.*

She hops up from her split and looks down at me because she's just super-way taller.

> *You can use your prodigy-level dance vision to help me—*

she makes a *whoosh* sound and opens her hands up like fireworks

> *—create an eleven-out-of-ten mind-blowing routine for callbacks, and* I'll *give* you . . .

she pauses and looks up into the tree's drooping branches and nods like the tree whispered something to her and then looks back down at me and finishes talking as if she never paused in the first place.

> *—the money my parents give me to pay for my solo dance lessons with Masterson.*

I'm trying to make sense of all those words when she adds, in a rushed breath:

> *Please.*
> *You know it and I know it . . .*
> *Masterson's crusty old choreo will sink me.*
> *Or at least sink my chances to get past—*

I must make a face because she flashes a blink-and-you'll-miss-it smile before she says,

> *—to get past the Competition That Shall Not Be Named . . . into the* Finals *That Shall Not Be Named.*

I don't say anything and Casey Price doesn't say anything.

The hot and humid breeze filtering through the tree branches reminds me of Ben Hur breathing in my face.

Casey Price taps her fingers on her popped hip again and then she shifts from one foot to the other until she looks away, past my face, up into the tree, sighs, and says,

Help me, JJ Johnson, you're my only hope.

I cough out a laugh and her eyes whip from the tree back down to me.

I point at her like she pointed at me earlier.

It was YOU!
Not Ms. J.
Who told Mr. Mann.
About FAM prelims.
YOU got me on the kudos list, didn't you?

Casey Price looks happy guilty.

She says:

No!

Then,

Maybe.

Then

Well . . .
You did such a good job, JJ.
And it didn't seem fair for no one to know that.
I mean, Veronica Verve basically lost her ability to speak when she watched you try out.
Shhh!
I know what you're about to say, and you should really just shut up.
Who CARES if she said you're a six out of ten dancer.
Did you not hear anything that came before or after that?
In all 14 seasons of FAA, she has never said anything like that to anyone.
Not even D'Andre, and he's her APPRENTICE CHOREOGRAPHER NOW.
She called you a prodigy, dummy!

I know Casey Price is trying to be nice, but I don't like being called a dummy, even in a nice way. And I don't like it when someone tells me to shut up, even in a nice way. And I don't like it when someone yells at me, even if they're saying possibly nice things.

I try to match Casey Price's volume, but it's tough to do because she is SO LOUD.

What does progedy even meeeeeeeeean?!

She steps back and shrugs in a very exaggerated way that STILL looks cool, which makes me even more mad for some reason and I don't even really know why I'm feeling so mad to begin with.

Casey Price screeches at me:

I don't knoooooooow!
But it HAS to be good, you dope!

I grab my backpack.

I'm not *a dope.*
Don't call me that.
Even if you're joking.
Also, my name is Jordan JACKSON.
Just like Ms. J, the librarian.
NO RELATION.

I stomp off, leaving Casey Price under the forest-bathing tree.

The hot breeze tumbles her yelling voice at me:

Well MY name is just Casey.
Not CaseyPrice*!*

Well, it IS Casey Price, but you don't always have
to say it all together like that!
It's just CASEY.

I keep stomping away, even faster now.

Casey Pr—CASEY keeps shouting.

Jordan Jackson!
Wait!
Come on!
Why are we yelling?

But I don't want to wait.
And I don't want to come on.
And I'm already late to old-lady art class.
Javier AND the Carol(e)s will be so far ahead of me.
And I still don't have all the supplies I need.
And I definitely just missed bus 315.

And sometimes I GUESS I DO LIKE YELLING.
Even though I don't like to be yelled AT.

But WHATever.

BRO TIME AT OLD-LADY ART CLASS

I'm in such a rush when I finally fly into old-lady art class, I smash open the door way too hard and it goes WHAM and one of the Carol(e)s goes *AHHH* and flings her paintbrush into the air.

Kat whips her head around and flings her hands up in front of her and I can't tell if she's trying to protect herself from my door wham or Carol(e)'s flying paintbrush, but either way, she still makes a yikes-face and lets out a kind of gruntingly surprised,

Whoaaaaaaaaa.

I say,

Sorry, sorry, Kat.
Sorry, sorry, everybody,

and my voice sounds squeaky and panicky like one of those little birds that get trapped inside hardware stores or airports.

I duck my head and hurry to my table even though I know ducking my head won't actually make me invisible like I wish it would.

I drop my backpack on the floor and flop in my seat and do some deep breathing because wow is it a longer run from the 310 bus stop than the 315 bus stop, and that's when Carole with an E pushes a chocolate chip cookie toward me across the table without looking up from her bird.

The late bird gets the gluten-free sand cookie.

Carol snorts without looking up from her bird, either, and says,

I didn't think they were sandy at all.

Carole with an E flicks her brush at her paper, making cool splatters near her bird's feet and says,

Maybe.
At least the cricket flour gives it some crunch.

I stop in mid-bite because wait . . . what? But I don't get a chance to splutter that question out loud because I feel a gentle whack on the back of my head and I turn around to see Javi fighting hard not to smile from within the cave of his hoodie hood.

Javi walks around the table, standing behind the Carol(e)s so he can look at their birds, and so he can glance up at me without them seeing and silently mouth,

Yum.

I try to be polite and finish my bite of the cricket flour sand cookie because you're always supposed to be polite when old people give you treats, that is a lesson I learned from going to Mom's newsroom when she still had a job and her white-haired editor would give me tan candy that tasted like my great-grandma used to smell and I would have to say *thank you* instead of *GROSS*.

My mouth is so dry from all the running and breathing, though, that I only manage to rearrange the cricket sand in my mouth and somehow make it even drier.

Kat appears out of nowhere, standing next to Javi behind the Carol(e)s and she's saying something about *great texture* and as soon as everyone's eyes are all on Carole with an E's splattered bird, I spit out the cricket cookie bite into my hand and slowly sprinkle the bits on the floor.

Kat sing-songs,

> *I'm looking forward to seeing what you create today, Jordan.*

My head pops up to catch her stare just as my mouth pops out,

> *Me, too!*

Javi's in his seat now and he hands me a piece of watercolor paper and a brush before I can even ask for it and right here in this very moment my whole self fills with a kind of warm glow to know that Javi is my actual real friend, not just a school friend or a Sandbox friend.

I bump his shoulder with my shoulder and say,

Who's ready for some bro time?

At exactly the same time, and without looking up from their birds, both Carol(e)s say,

I am!

Javi spews out a laugh so fast and loud and hiccup-y sounding that the rest of us crack up so hard we almost fall out of our chairs.

Kat gives everyone a ten-minute warning for the end of class, and even though I didn't have a chance to start painting, and even though I ate a bite of a cricket cookie, and even though I was worried Javier would be really mad at me for being so late, I'm still super glad I made it to old-lady art class today.

Javi knocks into my shoulder as we walk out together and says,

Th-think you'll ever actually m-make any art *in art class?*

I knock into his shoulder and add a little pop-and-lock arm move to jazz things up.

Only if it's bro-time art.

Javier laughs and says,

W-what is br-bro-time art?

The Carol(e)s speed-walk past us, and Carole with an E holds open the big front door that leads to the parking lot while Carol looks back at us and says,

I know you didn't ask,
but you want to know what I think?
I think bro-time art isn't a question at all.

Carole with an E snaps and smiles and points at Carol and then at me and Javi as we walk through the door into the steam of a fading afternoon.

She calls after us, pointing with both hands,

Bro-time art is an answer!
To so many things!
Stick THAT in your hat and think about it!

I don't know what those Carol(e)s are talking about, but I like how happy they sound when they say it.

Javier and I wave bye to them and Javi whispers to me,

If y-you were an old l-lady, I b-bet y-you'd be a C-Carol(e).

I don't really know what that's supposed to mean, either, but I'm taking it as a compliment.

I'm here!

WHERE IS JORDAN?

KAT KEEPS LOOKING OUT THE WINDOW (PROBABLY LOOKING FOR JORDAN)

JAVIER IS CURIOUS ABOUT WHERE JORDAN IS, TOO.

bird?

EVEN THE CAROL(E)S ARE WONDERING. WHO WILL EAT ALL THEIR SNACKS?

I will!

Sorry! Casey Price yelled at me under the tree and I missed the bus

:(

You know what time it is? It's Javi + Jordan BRO time!

What do you want to bro about?

ALL THE WAYS TO FIGURE OUT WHAT PROGEDY MEANS: A LIST BY JORDAN J

1. ask someone
    a. but what if it means something bad and the person telling me what it means feels bad about it meaning something bad so they make up what it means and I don't know if they're telling the truth because how would I know if I don't know what it means????
2. look it up on my phone
    a. find my phone
    b. charge my phone
3. look it up in a real dictionary like that giant one in the library at school

SCHOOL*

Usually, it's not that easy to get to school early because Mom is already at work and Dad doesn't drive until he's had at least two cups of coffee and one poop, so I have to take the 315 because the actual school bus doesn't come early enough to get to school early and also is disgusting and hot and no.

Now that Mom is laid off, though, she doesn't have to go to the newsroom anymore and she can do her new part-time job from home anytime, and because she hates her new part-time job more than anything (even driving me places!), she's always looking for other things to do instead of her new part-time job, like drive me to school early and act very excited that I asked to go to school early and make me wish I hadn't said anything so I could take bus 315 like I used to.

Probably, I should have listened to at least some of the questions she was asking me in the car, but ugh my brain is barely even awake yet and now I'm here at school and I can barely even remember getting here.

I have to stop in front of my locker and close my eyes and let Mom's echoing questions drain out of my ears so I can hear my ownself and my own questions, most importantly:

*Before school, in the library. I can't believe I spend so much time in the library!

Why did I want to get here early again?

I look at my new-and-improved to-do list of new and improved things to do.

Right!

I shove the list back in my pocket and walk to the library.

I want to look up the word *progedy*, but I don't want anyone to see me doing it or ask me about it or anything like that.

I want to look in a gigantic fancy dictionary and I want to read the definition on my own and I want to take as long as I need and read it over again if I need to and then I want to think about it by myself and figure out what Veronica Verve meant *all on my own.*

The best quietest place to do all that, and to (bonus!) find a gigantic fancy dictionary, is in the library before school.

I try to just wave and keep walking past Ms. J and toward the giant dictionary on the giant dictionary stand, but she looks at me in that way she does and her eyes attach to my face.

Jordan J, no relation! You're here early.

She whooshes over to me, her yellow caftan fluttering around her like butterfly wings. She keeps looking at me until her eyes pull words out of me.

Yeah, I wanted to get here early so I could look up a word in the giant cool dictionary that no one ever looks at.

I mean, I know I can look stuff up on my phone or whatever, I just thought it would be nicer or realer or something if I looked it up in an actual official old-fashioned book kind of dictionary, instead of having to trust that whatever I read on my phone is true and not just something made up by some internet dingleberry.

You know?

My words fly out and flop around in the air between us even though I didn't want to say ANY of them out loud.

Also, when did I stop walking?

Why am I just standing here in front of her?

Argh!

Ms. J's eyes stay locked on me and I swear they start to sparkle a little bit when she says,

Yes, I DO know what you mean.
I am so proud of you for being that astute about the internet.

I shrug as more words leap out of my mouth:

> *Oh, well, it's really my mom who's the smart one about that stuff.*
>
> *She's always complaining about people not fact-checking on the internet and how everyone says they're experts but really they're just experts at making stuff up on the internet and blah blah blah.*

Ms. J nods and sparkles and I wish she would stop talking, or stop making ME talk, because I've been standing here for kind of a long time and I'd really like to get to the dictionary. It takes me forever to read anything, and—

> *Come on!*
> *Let's go see what we can find!*

She starts to swoop off toward the big dictionary on its big dictionary stand, with her big caftan sleeves flapping like a happy stingray, but finally my brain and my words get it together and I say,

> *Wait, Ms. J.*
>
> *Do you, um, mind if I go use the dictionary by myself?*
>
> *I kind of want to* not *have any help while I find stuff and read it.*

That way I know I did it all by myself and that my understanding is my own and not just my understanding of someone else's understanding explained to me. Does that make sense?

Ms. J is frozen in place for a second, while she works to understand *my* meaning. Then she smiles her big warm sunshine smile that is honestly a little bit embarrassing to look at for some reason, and she says,

Absolutely, of course, that makes sense.
I'll be right here in case you have any questions, or need anything else.

I don't even nod or say thank you or anything, I just run off to the dictionary before it gets any later and other people start showing up and talking to me. Or vice versa.

There's one kind of yellow-y light shining down on the open dictionary like it's a piece of art or something and I feel weird touching such a big fancy book but Ms. J didn't tell me I couldn't touch it, so I try not to feel too weird.

The pages are very thin and almost see-through and I have to be really careful so I don't rip any of them as I turn big chunks of pages at a time to get to the *P* section.

(*P* section. Haha.)

Okay . . . let's see. . . .

Progenitor. No.

Progeny. Close, but no. Also, hold on a second.

It's really tricky to have to say the alphabet inside of words so you can find them in the dictionary. I think I might be in the wrong place?

I flip back and forth in the *P*s, but p-r-o-g-e-d-y isn't in here.

Maybe it has an *I* instead of an *E*?

Ugh, spelling doesn't make any sense at all.

I keep looking, but it's not anywhere.

Maybe a *J* instead of a *G*?

Project. No.

Projectile. No.

Skip, skip, skip . . .

ARGH. The bell is about to ring and I still haven't found this stupid word!

Did Veronica Verve make it up?

Hey, Jordan?

I didn't even notice Ms. J had snuck up on me. I also hadn't noticed I'd plopped my face into the middle of the dictionary.

Everything okay over here?
Did you find what you need?
Any questions for me before the bell rings?

Even though I didn't want help—I DON'T want help—I'm feeling kind of sad and desperate now so I guess I'm going to ask for help.

I can't find it.

My words blur into the wrinkled pages my face is crammed into.

I looked at all the p-r-o-g-e words and all the p-r-o-g-i words and all the p-r-o-j-e words and all the p-r-o-j-i words, and I can't find it anywhere.

I can feel some rustling around me which probably means Ms. J is standing closer now and maybe trying to look at the pages around my head.

I lift my face and look at Ms. J who is looking at me. I ask,

If it's a bad word is it even allowed in the dictionary?

Ms. J's head moves from side to side like she's trying to nod and shake her head at the same time.

Pretty much any and every word is allowed in the dictionary.

But sometimes new words aren't in there yet.
Is it a new word?

I shrug.

Is progedy a new word?

Ms. J's eyes tilt up to the ceiling while she thinks for a super-quick second, then she frowns and then she smiles and then she says,

Do you mean prodigy?
P-r-o-d-i-g-y?

Hmm.
I feel a tiny smile peek out of one side of my mouth.

Maybe I switched some letters around?

Ms. J starts flipping pages while she says,

Transposing letters happens all the time.
Your brain can do it when you read,
you can do it when you've only ever heard a
word said aloud, all sorts of reasons.

She stabs her finger on the page, looks up, and smiles at me.

There.
I'll let you read it and figure it out.
And if you have any questions, you know where
to find me.

Then she yells, *ACE! NO RUNNING IN THE LIBRARY!* so loud I jump about five feet straight up in the air while she swoops off to yell at Ace some more.

Finally. I'm all alone with the word Veronica Verve called me in front of a whole auditorium of people.

> **Prodigy** *(prod'əjē) n. pl.* **-gies.**
> ***1.*** *A person, especially a young one, endowed with exceptional qualities or abilities. Ex: "a Russian pianist who was a child prodigy in his day."* ***2.*** *An act or event so extraordinary or rare as to inspire wonder.* ***3.*** *An omen or portent. [Lat. prodigium, omen.]*

I read it a bunch more times so that all the words can jumble up in my brain and then relax next to each other, kind of like when Ms. Masterson has everyone on the dance team *shake it out* at the beginning of practice so that they can *leave their day behind and relax into the moves.*

I'm trying to relax into the meaning of the words as they relax into my brain and I don't even care that the bell rings which means I'll be late to class.

> ***1.*** *A person, especially a young one, endowed with exceptional qualities or abilities.*

I definitely know what most of those words mean, and stringing them together makes my heart beat faster.

> ***2.*** *An act or event so extraordinary or rare as to inspire wonder.*

My heart beats so fast I start breathing out of my mouth a little bit to try and slow it down.

> ***3.*** *An omen or portent.*

I don't really understand this part, but that's okay because the other parts are enough to help me figure out what Veronica Verve meant.

The yellow-y light shines down from the ceiling onto the definition of *prodigy* and it reminds me of the moment in the auditorium when the spotlight found *me* and I was still so upset I barely heard Veronica Verve call me a *choreography proge—prodigy.*

But I DID hear it.

And I DID hear everyone clapping and cheering.

And I can almost even remember all of *that* louder than I can remember *six out of ten, at best.* Except, I still don't understand how I can have the dance vision of a proge—prodigy but NOT be a good dancer. What!

I heave my backpack onto my shoulder while I let the word *prodigy* and its meaning—the meaning that I figured out all on my own—dance around in my brain.

I whisper it so I can hear how it sounds being born from my own voice.

The late bell rings as I walk toward the library doors, and Ms. J hollers at me from across the wide room,

Success?

I give her a smile and a thumbs-up before I hyper leap through the doors and out into the hallway. It might not be a ten out of ten outstanding hyper leap like Casey Pr—*Casey* could do, but that's okay because I'm a young person with *exceptional qualities or abilities so rare as to inspire wonder—*

Also, I *invented* that move. *I* did. By *myself.*

I add some skips and a pause for a baby freeze as I dance-walk to class.

You know, maybe I should find Casey Pr—*Casey*, and tell her she was right about *prodigy* being a good thing.

And maybe we could talk a little more about her whole pay-JJ-to-share-his-very-impressive-dance-visions idea.

I mean, she must *really* need some good dance-routine moves.

If I help Casey with her routine, I bet I can go to cxxxxxxxs with her, and if I get to go to callbacks with her, maybe I'll get to go backstage again, and if I get to go backstage again, maybe I can say hi to Veronica Verve, and maybe I can tell her that I figured out what prodigy means, and maybe I can ask her to please not play clown music when my six out of ten at best dance routine is on the show because, as we both know, prodigies are not clowns.

I'm a *prodigy*.
Veronica Verve said so herself.

I just really need to make sure she remembers that.
And Casey Price is my way in.

PROS AND CONS OF SHARING MY DANCE VISION WITH CASEY PRICE: A revised PRO AND CON LIST BY JORDAN J

Pro: my moves are exceptional

1. ~~what if my dance moves aren't good enough~~
2. what if my dance moves ARE good enough and Casey Price takes all the credit for them
3. what if I don't actually like her very much
4. what if she doesn't actually like ME very much
5. do you have to like each other to work together?
6. maybe not, but that wouldn't be very fun and I would be sad if dancing wasn't fun anymore
7. I would also be sad if teaching someone my dance moves wasn't fun because it seems like it would be really fun
8. is this a pro/con list?
9. I don't think it is
10. money

11. If I get to go to cxxxxxxxs with Casey I can say hi to VV and also ask very nicely for her to stop using clown music on the show because it makes people feel bad and feeling bad is the opposite feeling you're supposed to get from the show OR from dancing.

*Callbacks.

Dear Casey,

GUESS WHAT STARTS TODAY?

FAM PRACTICE WITH JORDAN J STARTS TODAY.

Meet me at the tree with droopy branches.

Please bring all your money.

haha! j/k

Not ALL of it.

Get ready to BOO your YAH.

Peace out,

Jordan J

FIERCE

ACROSS AMER

AFTER SCHOOL AT THE TREE WITH DROOPING BRANCHES

Casey's chin is pointed higher than usual and she is looking at me down the slope of her nose.

Finally she says,

So.

So I also say,

So.

And she says,

Are we doing this, or what?
My dance skills plus your dance vision?

And I say,

Plus your money?
Yes.
But don't call me dumb or dopey or yell at me, even if you are joking.

And she squints at me for a few seconds before she says,

Deal.
But don't run away like that again.

And I say,

Deal.

Casey makes a *whoosh* sound and opens her hands up like fireworks just like she did the other day.

Floating down from her hand is a ten-dollar bill.

I catch her ten dollars and her fireworks *whoosh* with a clap that springs back and turns into a little worm move that stretches from one arm to the next, and then without either of us saying anything Casey catches my worm move and mirrors it until she tosses the worm back at me.

We both laugh and it feels really nice to realize that Casey is a good dancer *and* a good person.

I think.

I add a couple of moves to the worm just to see what Casey will do with them and wow wow wow her arms and neck flow in a way that's so much better than good that I need Ms. J's gigantic dictionary to find some words to describe it.

My voice sounds a little like Ms. Masterson now when I say,

Show me what you have so far.
For your routine.
Maybe all you need is a little boo-yah to spice it up.

Casey doesn't say anything before she launches into a routine filled with a *lot* of dramatic ponytail swinging and a *lot* of dramatic neck rolls and a *lot* of slowly arcing high kicks that look like she's trying to clean a very big window with her flat foot.

It's . . . fine??

I don't even have to say anything when she's done. She just exhales and shakes her head.

See?

I don't want her to feel bad like I did when Veronica Verve told me I was a six out of ten, so I think for a minute before I say,

It's not bad.
It's just . . .

Casey interrupts me:

I know.
It's not bad.
But it's not fierce.
Erase all those moves from your brain, okay?
I want to see your dance vision.

She doesn't have to ask me again.

I show her about half a million ideas and she shows me half a million ways to make them even better and all of a sudden we're both super sweaty and out of breath, and I hear clapping and realize a small group of Rocketeers has gathered to watch us, which means Casey missed dance team practice and I missed *watching* dance team practice, and that means Casey is probably in big trouble with Ms. Masterson, and also that I've missed the 315 bus like five times over.

The small group of Rocketeers moves away toward a bunch of cars idling in the spot where parents wait to pick you up.

Casey seems to have realized how late it is, too, because she tosses her backpack over her shoulder with one hand and twists the end of her ponytail with her other hand.

You need a ride?

I'm still thinking about how to weave together a couple of hyper leaps and a reverse spin before I hear her question.

Do I need a ride?
What day is it again?
I honestly can't remember.

> *What day is it again?*

She laughs.

> *Today's Tuesday.*
> *Unless we just danced all night and now it's Wednesday.*

I must look super confused because she laughs harder and extra high-pitched, like probably a dolphin somewhere is looking around wondering who just said his name.

> *JJ.*
> *It's Tuesday.*
> *I promise.*

Aw, shiitake mushrooms.
Tuesday??
Tuesdays are art class with Javi.

Think I could get a ride to the community center?

Even before I'm finished asking I know that's not going to work.

I don't need a watch or a clock or a phone to tell me it's past 5:30, because the pink-and-orange sky is telling me that. Art class is 4:30 to 5:30 on Tuesdays, and I just missed the whole class.

Actually, a ride home would be super great if your mom or dad doesn't mind.

Casey holds her finger to her lips and motions for me to follow her allllllllll the way to the rickety old bleacher seats by the soccer field that flooded about seven thousand times before the Hart Rockets soccer team started practicing at the YMCA down the street.

It's starting to get dark now and I'm starting to get tired and I know Javier is going to be mad at me or sad because of me or both and I'm really, really starting to feel mad at me or sad because of me or both, too, and I don't really WANT to be following Casey to the old soccer field, which happens to be in the opposite direction of both the 315 bus and my house.

She runs behind the bleachers and reappears with an orange dirt bike that makes me hold my breath in a way I can't even explain.

She walks it over to me and asks,

> *Where do you live?*
> *I can't drive this on real roads, but luckily, I know almost all of the dirt roads and back ways in the whole town.*

Casey flips and clips her ponytail on top of her head, puts on a helmet covered in dried mud, and grins and looks like a totally different kid than the kid I just spent hours teaching hyper leaps and transition turns to.

> *Wait.*
> *YOU'RE going to take me home?*
> *On that?*
> *There's only one seat.*
> *Is it okay with your parents?*

I close my mouth and for a super-quick millisecond I feel like a huge dorky baby for asking all those questions, but then I go back to feeling like regular Jordan J, who definitely doesn't care that much about sounding dorky and who also definitely knows he's about to get on this dirt bike whether anyone's parents know or not.

Casey peers out at me through the open space in her helmet and I wonder if she ever gets rocks in her eyes and then I wonder why her helmet doesn't have a visor like a motorcycle helmet and then I wonder how I knew that *visor* was the right word. Good job, me!

She hands me a blue-and-white helmet crusted with dried mud and then she imitates me, which makes me feel like a line-mouth emoji.

> *I have a million brothers and sisters and my parents are always busy with work or my million brothers and sisters and I figured if I joined the dance team I wouldn't have to go home and babysit after school and it turns out I'm pretty good at dancing, so that worked out okay, and can you please stop asking me questions so that I can get you home before dark.*

Casey takes a deep breath and laughs.

> *Wow. That's hard to do in one breath.*
> *Are you coming or not?*
> *My ride is awesome, but it doesn't have any lights, so no night biking.*

I have decided to not be mad at her for making fun of me even though I didn't love it.

I put on the helmet even though I've never worn a helmet one time in my whole life.

It smells like socks and outside.

I tell her my address and climb behind her on the dirt bike and OMG Mom would have sixteen heart attacks if she saw this. *I* might actually have sixteen heart attacks, too, but the good kind of heart attacks, the kind you have when you float away from yourself for a second and watch yourself doing something you never thought you'd do and instead of feeling scared you feel like you could fly.

Casey turns to look at me, her grin lighting up the inside of her helmet.

All right, JJ, you ready?

I nod breathlessly, feeling my whole body vibrate as she kick-starts the bike and shouts:

Hold on tight!
We're about to fly!

And it really does feel like flying.
For real, not just in my mind.

MY DRIVEWAY

Just as I hop off the dirt bike and take off the helmet to hand to Casey, I hear the garage door open.

It slowly rises, revealing Mom bit by bit like we're in a movie and we're meeting either a superhero or a super villain for the first time.

Bare feet . . .
Tanned legs . . .
Cut-off jeans . . .
Hands on hips . . .
Striped shirt . . .
Mouth in a line and not in a smile . . .
Eyes squinting . . .

The garage door motor and the dirt bike motor both turn off at the same time and it gets really quiet really fast.

Except I can hear Ben Hur barking inside the house.

Mom walks closer to us and in a weirdly cheerful voice she says,

THIS is exciting!

I glance at Casey and then back at Mom.
Casey glances at me and then Mom.

Mom stares at the dirt bike and Casey and me all at the same time.

At least she isn't having sixteen heart attacks?

> *Hi there!*
> *I'm Jordan's mom.*
> *You can call me* Jordan's mom.
> *What's your name?*

Mom's weird voice is getting weirder by the second, and yeah, I think she IS having sixteen heart attacks; she's just having them in her guts instead of loud and mad in front of Casey.

Casey looks back at me and then at Mom and then laughs and says,

> *Jordan's friend?*

Mom's eyes get even squintier and she smiles that smile she smiles when she's suuuuuper mad but trying to be polite, like that one time a long time ago when she and Dad were at a parent-teacher conference and my teacher called me *special.*

I take a step back without even meaning to because that smile is a warning.

> *Jordan's friend, huh?*
> *This one has jokes!*

It's time for me to jump in and save Casey's life so I say,

> *Ha, ha, ha.*
> *This is Casey Price, Mom.*
> *I'm helping her with her Fierce Across America callbacks routine.*

Now Casey jumps in and says,

> *I'm actually* paying *Jordan.*
> *For his dance vision.*
> *Because his choreography is fire.*

I feel a little extra fire in my cheeks as we all stare at each other.

Casey doesn't move closer to Mom for a handshake or anything like that. She stays put by her bike and waves. Smart.

Mom motions to the dirt bike.

> *And who is this?*

Casey swings her big-helmeted head toward me, her confused eyes saying, *Uh—?*

> *I call handlebars!*

Oh great, now Dad is out here, too?? He has Ben Hur on a leash and Ben Hur is barking like she's going to fight the dirt bike in a battle to the death.

I don't know, Rock.
Are handlebars the passenger seat on a dirt bike?
I seem to recall dirt bikes having only ONE seat.
For the driver.
Who must legally be a certain age.

Casey says,

Well, actually, a hundred and twenty five cc moto like this one doesn't have any legal limits on age. As long as you don't ride it on actual roads.

Uh-oh.

Casey just *well, actually'd* Mom and that is a thing most humans know not to do.

Mom squeezes her chest with super-tight crisscrossed arms.

Dad holds out a treat to get Ben Hur to stop barking.

They both stare at me and Casey and the dirt bike.

How old are you—

sorry—

what was your name again?

Casey, Ma'am.

I'm thirteen.

Ma'am.

Mom laughs and it's loud and scary just like in those old movies about pirates or wars when someone shoots a loud and scary cannon as a warning to their enemy to get away fast.

She has jokes AND she's bold.

Dad clears a laugh from his throat and tries to look mad but Dad can never successfully look mad, so he just looks sort of like he's trying to fart very quietly.

Took a wrong turn at Well, actually, *Jordan's friend.*

And then another wrong turn at Ma'am, *I'm afraid.*

Mom points at me and then flings her hand at the garage.

You!

In the house!

And you—

She points her face at Casey—

I'm really sorry, but WHAT is your name again?

Casey Price, Ma—

To be honest, Casey Price, I'm not sure we should let YOU drive away on this thing.

Taking Mom's cue perfectly, Casey jumps on the bike, cranks it until the engine rumbles so loud I can feel it in my chest, then waves at me and yells over the noise,

See you tomorrow, JJ!
I promise to practice those leaps before, uh . . . practice!

Casey squeals off and the squeals are extra squeeeeeeealy, which seems to be *a poor choice in the moment,* to use words Mom likes to use.

Dad gives Ben Hur her treat and says,

Cool bike.
Absolutely very dangerous.
And absolutely not okay for you to ride without proper equipment or training.
Or permission.
Nonetheless . . .
Very cool bike.

Also, very cool boss.
High-five for getting a job.

I high-five Dad and breathe out,

Thanks.

Mom shakes her head like she just cannot believe she lives in the same world with the rest of us and then she looks up at the blue sky, takes a deep cleansing breath, and says,

Javier's mom was just here.
I'm sure you know why.

I look down at my muddy feet because I do know why.

She left something for you from Javi.

Mom walks through the garage and opens the door into the kitchen, holding it for me as I walk through.

I know I don't need to say this, but I'm going to say it anyway:
Javier's feelings are hurt, Jordan.
And Dad and I were worried you were kidnapped or dead in a ditch or something.

MOM! Don't say stuff like that!

Well, kiddo, what happens if you fall off that dirt bike?
You'll probably fall into a—

Mom points to Dad, who points back at Mom, and then at the same time they say,

DITCH.

Except Dad actually says *RAVINE* and not *DITCH* and then Mom says *Ravine*? and at the exact same time Dad corrects himself and says *Ditch* and they are both not smiling even though I can tell they want to be smiling and omg do they think they're a comedy duo or something?

Mom nods very seriously and says in a low voice,

A ditch.
And who's going to pay THAT hospital bill, Jordan?
Casey Price?
I doubt it.

Dad puts his arm around me and we all walk into the house together even though Ben Hur only got a five-second walk down half the driveway. His voice is very serious when he says,

Did Casey Price say anything about a comprehensive benefits package to go with your new job?

I look up and see the joke-y sparkle in Dad's eye which is a little bit comforting even though I know I'm still in trouble.

Mom flings her arms to the side and yells very dramatically,

> *I'm thirty-seven, and even I don't have a job with benefits!*

Carolina looks up from the kitchen table as we all walk in. She has half a donut in her mouth and sprinkles crumbs when she shrugs and says,

> *I don't have a job with benefits either, and I'm NINE!*

Dad unleashes Ben Hur and hands me a folded piece of paper that must be the note from Javi that his mom dropped off. He shakes his head and fights off a small smile.

> *It's a tough world, that's for sure.*
> *But at least it . . .* benefits *. . . us all to know that so young.*

Mom rolls her eyes and tries really hard not to laugh.

> *Rock, no.*
> *Just . . .*
> *That's not even a joke.*

I join in because it's always fun to gang up on Dad especially if ganging up on Dad distracts everyone from being mad at *me.*

Yeah, Dad. That barely made any sense at all.

Dad snaps a kitchen towel at me and I scream and laugh while he pretends very badly to be mad and says,

YOU don't make any sense.

He snaps the towel at Mom next which is an even worse idea than Casey making her dirt bike tires squeal in front of Mom.

YOU don't make any sense either.

Mom uses her lightning-fast Mom reflexes and grabs the towel before it can snap her and she yanks it from Dad's hands and snaps it at him which makes him squeal almost as loud as Casey, and they are making way too much noise now, so I take a couple of dinner donuts and go to my room.

MY BEDROOM*

*Well, Javi made this at old-lady art class bro time, but I am just seeing it now in my not-old-lady, not-art-class, not-bro-time bedroom.

STILL MY BEDROOM

Uh . . . hello?
Is this a time traveler from the olden days who doesn't understand texting?

Hey, Ben Y, sorry to call you on the phone so late like I am a robot or time traveler, but I need your help and I'm way too tired to type words.

What's up?

Javi is mad at me and I feel bad for making him mad and I won't be able to sleep until I fix it or have a plan to fix it but I don't know how to fix it because I don't have Javi Vision like I have Dance Vision and—

Duuuude.
Slow down.
As Ms. J says, help me help you.
What even IS Javi Vision?

You know. It's like Dance Vision. But Javi Vision.

I do not know.
But please, go on . . .

Argh! Ben Y! You have to help me help you help me!

I said GO ON!

I AM GOING ON. Okay, so Dance Vision is like feelingknowingbelievingseeing instead of regular plain seeingseeing. It's how I know when to pop, how I feel when to squat, how I believe it will work even before I ever see any of it with my actual eyeballs.

Sooooo, Javi Vision is like Dance Vision but . . . broken! If my Javi Vision worked as well as my Dance Vision, I would know exactly how to say, You're totally my bro, Javi, *and I'd also know exactly when to say,* I'm sorry, dude, *and then I'd figure out how to get all those words to dance together so that, boom, Javi would feelknowbelievesee how much I feelknowbelievesee all those things. . . . Ben Y? Hello?*

You know what I think, Jordan?

What?

I think you need to remember Javier is a human person and not a pop or a squat. Have you even talked to him about any of this? You can't just feelknowbelievesee what to fix with a human person. You have to talk to Javi and listen to what he says. It takes two to tango or whatever.

So . . . I need Javi Hearing instead of Javi Vision?

Probably a good place to start.

Ben Y?

Yeah?

Did you just help me help you help me by helping me from myself, while ALSO helping us both understand tango rules a little better?

Good night, Jordan.
And you're welcome.

Do you think you have Jordan Vision, Ben Y?

Goodniiiiiiiight, Jordaaaaaan.

Goodnight, Ben Y.
Thank youuuuuuuu.

ACTUAL CALLBACKS

THINGS MO MIGHT SAY ABOUT THE FEELINGS I'M HAVING ABOUT NOT DANCING AT CALLBACKS BUT STILL BEING AT CALLBACKS BECAUSE I SHARED MY DANCE VISION WITH CASEY: A LIST BY JORDAN J

1. is there a more descriptive word you could use instead of *jealous*?
2. do you have any positive feelings about Casey's dancing?
3. will you remember to not eat the nachos this time because they really hurt your stomach at prelims?
4. can you remind Casey that you're very proud of her no matter what?
5. can you remind yourself that you're very proud of yourself no matter what?
   a. even if you eat the nachos anyway because they taste so good and the cheese is so gooey?

OUTSIDE FRESHWATER'S FAMOUS DING DARLING AUDITORIUM

I'm not going to stay.
That's okay, right?

Mom pulls up to the drop-off area at FAM callbacks and my stomach spins a little bit because I didn't think about how callbacks would be at the same auditorium where I found out I'm only a *six out of ten, at best* dancer.

That's okay.

I get out of the car and before I shut the door Mom yells,

Text me when you're done.
Do NOT ride that dirt bike home, you hear me?

I shut the door and start to walk away, pretending I didn't hear her because I REALLY want to ride Casey's dirt bike home, but then I turn around and wave. I also REALLY want Mom to smile at me.

The front of the Building That Ruined Everything stares at me and the automatic sliding doors open and close and open and close like the building is whispering to me: *I've already eaten you up and swallowed your dreams and spit you out. Why are you back? You don't belong here!*

I see Casey waving at me from inside, so I walk through the doors and let the building swallow me up again.

INSIDE FRESHWATER'S FAMOUS DING DARLING AUDITORIUM*

The crowd is so loud while Casey dances, it's like every single person who's here is here to see her. Like, it doesn't even matter that Casey's mom and dad and million brothers and sisters aren't here, and it doesn't matter that only a couple of Rocketeers who were in line early enough to get first-come-first-serve-free tickets are here, because there are STRANGERS here cheering for Casey as if they know her and love her.

It's weird to feel so happy and excited but also feel kind of . . . the opposite of that, all at the same time.

I mean, Casey TOTALLY out-fierced herself onstage. She took my dance vision and gave it *life*. She tore it up out there and I screamed and cheered and clapped along with everyone else.

But . . .

But . . .

But . . .

*A few hours later because we had to wait for Casey's number to be called and for all the TV-show people to get their TV stuff ready and for all the dancers before Casey to dance their routines, which were all really fierce, wow.

Now I'm in the hallway waiting for Casey to make her way off-stage, and I imagine her winding through the dark backstage area, and I bet she's still a little out of breath and I also bet she's following the lady with the black eyeliner who's lighting the way with her tiny flashlight, and . . .

My lips flutter out a sad fart noise.

It's not that I'm *not* happy about how fierce Casey danced.

I am!

It's not that I'm *not* proud of all my dance moves that she electrified up there.

I am!

But also?

I wanted to be fiercely dancing under the bright hot stage lights.

I wanted to electrify my *own* dance moves up there.

I make another sad fart noise as I slide my back down a wall and sit on the itchy carpet and wait for Casey to appear.

I think I understand now what Veronica Verve means when she tells someone they danced so well, it hurt her feelings.

It's weird to be this happy and not actually very happy at all.

Jordan!

Casey leaps toward me. I wave so she knows it's me, even though she must know it's me because she yelled my name.

When she gets closer I yell,

CASEY PRICE!
YOU MAGNIFICENT SON OF A BENCH!

A bunch of people turn around to look at us and laugh. Casey laughs, too, and slides her back down the wall to sit next to me. She knocks her knees into mine.

I thought we've been over this.
Casey.
Cay-see.
Say it with me:
Caaaaaay-seeeeeeee.
No Price.
Only say Price *if you're taking attendance.*

I know.
I can't help it.
I just like how it sounds.
It's like the name version of jazz hands.

Casey laughs and it's extra extra loud bouncing around the lobby's high ceiling.

You have a very strange brain, JJ.

I know that, too.

Neither one of us says anything for a minute, and the noises from all around the lobby fill the quiet space around us.

So?

Casey nudges my knee with her knee again.

How WAS it??

A guy in a purple unitard walks by, looks down at us, and says,

FIERCE, GIRL.
That's how it was!

We laugh and do some air high fives with him as he keeps walking past.

I knock Casey's knee with mine this time.

That guy is one hundred percent right.
You were the fiercest of the fierce, Caaaaaay-seeeeeee.
You ate everyone's lunch.

Casey closes her eyes and leans her head against the wall.

You think?

I do the same thing.

Yes.
I do think.

She turns her head toward me and whispers,

How come you don't seem very happy about it, then?

My eyes stay closed and I hope my eyelids can hold in the tears that I feel filling up my eyeholes. I whisper back,

I'm totally happy about it.

Casey turns her head away from me and leans it against the wall again.

Are you, though?

Yes.

I don't believe you.

Why not?

Because you never speak in one-word sentences.

Never?

What's wrong, JJ? What did I mess up?

You didn't mess up anything, Casey.

You're sure?

One million percent sure.

Then why are you acting sad-weird instead of regular Jordan-weird?

Neither one of us says anything for a while, then Casey stands up. She reaches her hand down to pull me up next to her.

Do you want to get a snack? I'm starving.

Okay.

You're kind of freaking me out, dude.

Sorry.

We eat our nachos and get swarmed by the Rocketeers who stood in line for THREE HOURS to get in, and who drip cheese on the table while they wave their arms around and describe the other auditions they saw.

While everyone talks and bounces around us like excited puppies, Casey laughs her hot-pink laugh and talks with them and I keep looking at the giant clock on the wall to see if it's time for the Fierce Finals list to be posted.

It keeps being not.

Maybe once the list is posted I'll figure out a way to find Veronica Verve and say hi and maybe she'll remember me and maybe she'll even be happy to see me, and we can talk about how Casey's dancing is so good and clown music is so terrible and then VV and JJ will be VVJJBFFs and I will finally feel better about everything, and it will have been totally worth it to come to callbacks even though I didn't get to dance or be on stage at all. Maybe.

FIERCE ACROSS AMERICA

Season 15

Dear #0156,

Thank you for your participation in *Fierce Across America*'s groundbreaking 15th season.

Without dancers like you, our show would be just another competition show. It's your talent, your spark, and your passion that put the *Fierce* in *Fierce Across America*.

Congratulations—YOU HAVE MADE IT TO FINALS!

We look forward to seeing you back here at the DING DARLING AUDITORIUM in SEVEN days.

You Are Fiercely Loved,

Mae

Veronica

PLEASE TUNE IN ON WEDNESDAYS THIS SUMMER,
8 P.M. EST/7 P.M. CST, TO WATCH THE YOUNGEST, FIERCEST
COMPETITORS EVER DANCE FOR THEIR LIVES.

OUTSIDE FRESHWATER'S FAMOUS DING DARLING AUDITORIUM

Sure you don't want a ride home?

Casey cranks the dirt bike and makes it roar and in a split second I say yes instead of no, even though I know Mom will eat me alive if she finds out.

Casey shouts over her shoulder:

If your mom hunts me down and murders me for letting you ride on my dirt bike, it's totally your fault.

I put on her extra helmet and hop on the bike and we fly away away away.

My arms are wrapped under Casey's arms and my chest is full of rumbles and the noise of the bike vibrates inside my helmet until it shakes out all my thoughts and I squeeze Casey tighter with one arm so I can fling my other arm out to the side.

My palm cuts through the wind, catching cool splashes of mud that sting when they first hit.

I pull my arm out of the wind and grab onto Casey just as she drives the bike up a steep heap of dirt and we fly up into the air—like literally fly into the actual air—with no wheels on the ground.

Everything slows down at the same time as everything speeds up which makes no sense but that's how it is.

I squeeze Casey extra hard because I don't want to fall off especially if we're flying in the actual air, and I can tell that Casey is holding her breath and maybe it's because I'm squeezing so hard or maybe it's because she doesn't want to fall off either.

The bike shifts in midair, pointing down toward the ground now, instead of up toward the sky, and my rear end starts to lift up off the back of the seat and my weight presses into Casey's back as gravity grabs us both and pulls us down, and then . . .

WHAM

. . . the bike slams into the ground and my butt slams into the seat and one of my arms shakes loose from squeezing Casey, but somehow the other one is still holding onto her so I don't spin off like trash flying out of the bed of a pickup truck.

For the first time ever I feel more scared of Casey's dirt bike than of Mom finding out I've been riding Casey's dirt bike.

But then, somehow, my arm swings back and I fling it around Casey and I feel her lungs expand in a huge breath, and that's enough to dissolve my scaredness into bits of relieved puffs of breath that fly out behind us and get lost in the cloud of dust we leave behind.

Casey steers this live-wire lightning bolt toward the pond near my house where I can get off and walk the rest of the way, and it's like nothing else exists except for me and Casey and the wind and the bike and this exact bubble of a moment that might last one more second or forever, I can't really tell anymore.

HOME

Mom's eyes get all big and shiny when I walk in the front door.

Wellllll??????

I try to make myself sound as happy as I wish I actually felt.

She did it!
Finals!
Next week.
Sweet.

Mom side-eyes me while she gets the ice cream out of the freezer.

What happened.

She doesn't even say it like a question; she says it like she knows something definitely happened to make me act all extra-Jordan-y like this.

I shrug.

It was great.
She did great.
Everyone cheered.

Mom side-eyes me from the other side as she scoops ice cream into bowls.

And?

I side-eye her back.

And, I don't know?
I want to be happy about it.
I AM happy about it.
I just . . .

I shrug again.

I really wanted to see Veronica Verve again.
I wanted to say hi and see if she remembered me.
And if she did, I wanted to ask her a question.
But I didn't see her at all,
except for way off in her seat,
where no one else can go.

Mom side-eyes me and says,

Is it something you can ask me?
I don't know anything about dance, but I do know—

My mouth shouts before my brain thinks.

No!
Mom!
Duh!
You can't answer every question in the world!

Mom looks out the kitchen window and doesn't side-eye me. She presses her mouth in a line before she says,

Well.
I'm glad Casey did so well.
I know you both worked really hard.

I agree with all those things Mom just said and yet for some reason I just want to yell at her more and be really mad out loud and maybe slam a door.

A door slams as if I made it happen with my brain, but I didn't. It's just Dad and Carolina coming home from Food World.

Dad plops a couple of bags on the counter and rubs his hands together.

Ice cream!
That seems promising. . . .
How did it go, kiddo?

Ugh. I don't want to talk about it anymore so I grab the whole ice cream container and go to my room.

Carolina shouts, *RUDE*, after me, and Dad says, *I have to agree with you, sport. That WAS rude.*

Mom says,

I think he rode on that dirt bike again, too.

I don't hear anything else because this time I slam the door with my actual hand and it feels very, very satisfying.

HOME*

The clock on the microwave says 3:23 a.m. when I sneak into the kitchen to get some ice cream so I can sneak back into the living room and eat Chocolate Chip Monster Delight while I watch old recordings of *Fierce Across America*.

Ben Hur curls up in my lap, soft and warm and breathing calmly while I fast-forward and rewind and fast-forward and rewind, looking for all the clown music parts in all the seasons.

I need to see just exactly how bad the dancers were when they got the clown music. Was my *six out of ten, at best* prelims routine better or worse than theirs?

What if all my friends watch the premiere and they see me on TV with clown music playing while Veronica Verve yells *NO CALLBACKS* at me?

What if Ms. J sees it?

What if the Rocketeers see it?

What if Mom and Dad and Carolina see it?

What if Ms. Masterson sees it and it makes her happy because it would mean I'm a clown dancer and my Boo-Yah Report for

*The middle of the night, all alone, while everyone else is snoring.

the newspaper is just some dumb kid talking about dumb things he doesn't know anything about?

I eat more ice cream and fast-forward and rewind and fast-forward and rewind and somewhere in my brain I can juuuuust barely hear a voice trying to remind me about being a prodigy, but it's being drowned out by a louder voice pointing out that no one deserves to be made fun of on TV, whether they are a prodigy or not.

I try to match my breathing with Ben Hur's sleepy breathing so I don't spin off into the most x-treme Jordan-ing of all Jordan-ings.

Our breathing becomes the backbeat to the audience slow-clapping along with Mae Michaelson as Season Five Fan Favorite Jamie Wu finishes dancing for his life. No clown music there.

Now our breathing and the slow-clapping join with some *bleeeerping* frogs out in the backyard and the sounds all mix together in a calming rhythm.

My eyes close and my brain chants:

You're a prodigy, not a clown.
You're a prodigy, not a clown.
You're a prodigy, not a clown.
You're a prodigy, not a clown.

I dream that I'm writing a letter to Mo. I'm trying to explain to her that I looked in the dictionary again, and this time next to the word *prodigy,* it said: *exceptional clown.*

And Mo's voice booms over me:

> *Do you want to say more about that, Jordan?*
> *Would you like to explain the clown music that follows you everywhere, Jordan?*
> *Jordan?*
> *Jordan?*

My eyes pop open.

Dad is kneeling next to me, gently shaking my shoulder.

> *Jordan?*
> *Kiddo?*
> *What are you doing in here?*
> *Did you eat ALL the ice cream?*
> *Let's get you to bed.*

Dad tucks me into bed just like he did when I was little and he kisses me on the forehead and I whisper, *Boo-yah* and Dad whispers, *You're ten out of ten outstanding at eating ice cream, kiddo,* and I snuggle under my covers and try not to dream about anything at all.

MY BEDROOM

I pretend to be sick even though Mom and Dad and Carolina and probably even Ben Hur all know that I am not actually sick.

> *Can I stay home from school?*

I stop pretending to be sick and I sneak back to my room to eat a donut while Mom and Dad argue about letting me stay home and as soon as Carolina yells, *NO FAIR,* and I hear the door shut, I know that Dad won the argument.

There's a soft knock on my bedroom door and yep. Dad.

> *Want to talk about it, kiddo?*

I shake my head.

> *This is your one free pass, okay?*
> *Back to school tomorrow, right?*

I nod even though I am planning to avoid Casey for much longer than just today, and that means I need a better plan than hiding in my bedroom.

< Newspaper Typing Club Chat >

JORDANJMAGEDDON!!!! ENTERS CHAT

BenBee: Wait.

BenBee: Where are you, Jordan?

JORDANJMAGEDDON!!!!: I logged onto the server from home.

JORDANJMAGEDDON!!!!: I'm sick.

JORDANJMAGEDDON!!!!: Cough cough.

0BenwhY: If you're sick, why are you awake this early?

0BenwhY: And why would you log onto anything having to do with school??

0BenwhY: (even *if* it's Sandbox-related)

JORDANJMAGEDDON!!!!: idk

JORDANJMAGEDDON!!!!: I like playing Sandbox with you y'alls.

JORDANJMAGEDDON!!!!: Even if it's at school. And I'm not.

BenBee: You got kudo'd AGAIN, dude. Can't believe you missed it!

jajajavier:): Jordan misses a lot of things these days.

JORDANJMAGEDDON!!!!: I got kudo'd again? Why?

0BenwhY: Mr. Mann said you and Casey advanced to finals.

JORDANJMAGEDDON!!!!: WHAT!!!

JORDANJMAGEDDON!!!!: I did not. Only Casey advanced.

BenBee: Yeah, but you've been helping her, right?

BenBee: Dance training, or whatever, right?

BenBee: And she wouldn't have made it to finals without you, right?

BenBee: You're a team, right?

JORDANJMAGEDDON!!!!: I guess.

JORDANJMAGEDDON!!!!: Sort of.

JORDANJMAGEDDON!!!!: yeah.

BenBee: Then that means your TEAM made it to finals, duh!

BenBee:

BenBee: Too bad you're sick, everyone at school is pretty excited about all this.

jajajavier:): He's not sick.

JORDANJMAGEDDON!!!!: Yes I am! COUGH! COUGH!

0BenwhY:

JORDANJMAGEDDON!!!!: I just . . . I'm not ready to see Casey yet.

JORDANJMAGEDDON!!!!: Even though I'm super happy for her.

JORDANJMAGEDDON!!!!: I'm afraid my face might not look super happy when I see her.

JORDANJMAGEDDON!!!!: And that makes me feel bad.

JORDANJMAGEDDON!!!!: And bad is another word for sick.

0BenwhY: OMG WHY ARE WE NOT ACTUALLY PLAYING SANDBOX. THIS IS THE BEST PART OF MY DAY AND I WANT TO BUILD NEW

CHAT INFRACTION

JJ11347 ENTERS CHAT

JJ11347: Excuse me for interrupting, but I was reading over Ben Y's shoulder

0BenwhY: Hey!

JJ11347: and I wanted to pop in to congratulate you, Jordan.

JJ11347: I realize you're upset that you aren't dancing in the finals for your show, but Ben B is right.

BenBee: EXCUSE ME WHAT CAN SOMEONE PRINT THAT OUT PLEASE?????

BenBee: 🏆 ✓ A+ 💯

JJ11347: Ben B, please.

JJ11347: You've created a partnership with Casey, Jordan.

0BenwhY: Gross.

JJ11347: CAN I TYPE WITHOUT BEING INTERRUPTED, PLEASE?

0BenwhY: ugh. sorry.

BenBee: Sorry for interrupting. I'm still right, though, right?

JJ11347: It's a special calling to be a person in this world who finds success by helping others find their ow

CHAT INFRACTION

JORDANJMAGEDDON!!!!: Huh?

JJ11347: It's like Sandbox, a little bit, if you think about it.
JJ11347: Casey succeeds because you have created the tools she needs to find that success.

BenBee: Like Ben Y teaching her potion to Ms. J so Ms. J could melt those ghosts!

JJ11347: Exactly.

JORDANJMAGEDDON!!!!: I'm the potion-maker?

JJ11347: Yes.

0BenwhY: Casey is Ms. J?

JJ11347: Uh . . . yes.

jajajavier:): Who are the ghosts, then?

BenBee: The other dancers?

JJ11347: MY POINT IS THIS.
JJ11347: You are a teacher, Jordan, and that is a gift.

0BenwhY: omg make it stop. someone spray her with a water bottle.

JJ11347: What?? It IS.
JJ11347: Darn. There's the bell.
JJ11347: Please think about what I said, Jordan.

JORDANJMAGEDDON!!!!: I make dance potions for Casey to kill dancer ghosts?

JJ11347: You are a gifted teacher with a student who needs you.
JJ11347: See you back at school tomorrow?

JORDANJMAGEDDON!!!!: yes?

JJ11347: Fabulous!

OLD-LADY ART CLASS BRO TIME WITH JAVIER

You were right.
I'm not sick.
I had a one-day pass from Dad to miss school.

I flop down next to Javi, who is already working on his bird because I guess he got here early or started it at home or something.

Y-you s-sure y-you're not s-sick?
S-something must be w-w-wrong
if y-you're here on t-time.

Javi's hoodie hood is pointed down at the bird he's painting, so I bend around to peer into it so I can see what his face looks like because his words don't sound very smiley, and yep, just like I thought, no smiles to be found anywhere.

Nothing's wrong, Javi.
It's old-lady art class bro time!
Why would anything be wrong?
Just because I'm early?
There's nothing wrong about that.
In fact, all is right about that.
Ha! See?
Everything's all right!

The Carol(e)s slide into their seats at the other side of the table and act like they're talking to each other instead of talking to us, even though they are totally talking to us.

Carol says,

> *You know, if someone has to say the words* all right *more than once, it's usually an indication that things are not, in fact, all right.*

Carole with an E says,

> *Agreed.*

Then she takes the foil off the plate in front of her, revealing a pile of very pale and disgusting-looking brownie-shaped . . . things. And she says,

> *Blondie?*

And I can't help but say,

> *What?*

And Carole with an E says,

> *Blondie.*
> *It's like a brownie but without chocolate.*

Javier pipes up and says,

Wh-who w-w-wants a-a-a—

He closes his eyes and before either of the Carol(e)s can interrupt him, I look at them and hold up my hand for them to wait because Javier really, really hates it if you finish his sentences for him, especially if he's already halfway through.

After a few more seconds of wrestling with his words, Javi opens his eyes and says,

b-b-brownie wi-without chocolate?

Without any pause at all, Carol smiles and says,

My point exactly.
How is anything ever all right in a world where
chocolate-less brownies exist?

And now I know something definitely IS wrong because Javi's stutter struggle is real right now, and when Javi's stutter struggle gets real like this it usually means he's stressed out or mad or otherwise freaking out about something.

Everyone keeps eating blondies, even though they're brownies without chocolate, and none of us says another word for the entire art class, not even me which is also usually a sign that something is wrong.

It only takes six blondies before I throw up.

where's the
bird part of
your bird, Javi?

DON'T WRITE ON
MY BIRD

BUT THESE ARE
ONLY LEGS

DON'T WRITE
ON MY BIRD LEGS,
JORDAN.

How are we
going to bro it
out if you don't
talk to me w/your
voice or on
your bird
legs?

Javi, are you mad at me?

I'M GOING TO HAVE
BRO TIME WITH CARA
AND CAROLE.
LIKE I USUALLY DO.

OUTSIDE*

Ben Hur pulls and pulls and pulls at her leash, and I let her drag me toward the mucky pond in the back of the neighborhood.

As soon as we get to the pond, I notice a silent orange blur bouncing along the opposite side, heading right for us.

Uh-oh.
Is that Casey?
Do dirt bikes have a stealth mode?

The orange blur bounces closer until Casey pulls up next to me, riding a regular leg-powered bike that sprays out a rainbow of mud as she twists it into a sudden stop.

*It's sometime in the afternoon the day after old-lady art class bro time, but I don't know exactly what time because I haven't been to school in two days** and time doesn't feel like it really exists if I'm not in school.

I only had one free pass from Dad, but then I ate six blondies at old-lady art class because Javier wouldn't talk to me and I didn't know what else to do with my mouth and those blondies made me barf* so Mom let me stay home from school again in case I was actually sick.

***I didn't tell Mom about the blondies (or about Javier being mad), only the barf.

Ben Hur barks and growls and darts around, while Casey drops the bike and takes off her helmet.

> *It's okay, Ben Hur. That's just Casey. You've met her before, remember?*

Casey grabs her heart in pretend shock.

> JUST *Casey?*
> *Is that all I am to you,* JUST *Casey?!*
> *After everything we've been through together?*

Ben Hur keeps barking and Casey kneels next to her so Ben Hur can smell her easier.

> *It's okay, Ben Fur.*
> *I'm a nice Casey.*

A tiny tiny smile tries to make a crack in my sad.

Did Casey just say Ben *FUR*?
That is *such* a better name.
How did I not think of that name?
Ben *FUR*!

Once Ben Fur stops going bonkers and starts chewing Casey's shoelaces, Casey stands and puts her hands on her hips.

So?
Where have you been, dude?
Fierce Finals are happening in one hot second, and
yet . . . you totally did the thing you said you wouldn't do!
And I can't figure out what would make you do that.
You're a lot of things, Jordan, but you aren't a person
who says one thing and does another.
At least, not until now.
Am I not paying you enough?
I have more money now.

Casey fishes a wad of money out of her shorts pocket, and shoves it at me.

Here's a bonus for getting us to Finals.
Plus an advance for the next couple practices.

I take the wad from her and shove it in my own pocket and I can't seem to look at her, so I watch Ben Hur switch from eating shoelaces to eating a stick.

Casey kicks at some weeds and watches Ben Hur, too.

I wish I could pay you what you're worth,
but that wad of cash is as close to a gagillion
dollars as I can get.

She looks up and tries to laugh, but it sounds more like a cough.

> *Anyway.*
> *Are we cool now?*
> *Can we get back to work?*

I don't know enough words to find the right ones to explain why I've been avoiding her, and how avoiding her has nothing to do with when or how much she pays me, but everything to do with when or how much I've been feeling sad.

I don't want Casey to think I'm sad because of her, because I'm NOT sad because of her. I'm just feeling my feelings like Mo says it's okay to do and those feelings are A LOT right now.

Hopefully, my sad and jealous feelings will all be felt soon and I can also stop worrying about the clown music and I can *also* also try out feeling some excited feelings about my ownself.

I slap a mosquito on my arm and a little splotch of blood blooms like a flower in my sweat.

Casey rubs the back of her neck and keeps squinting at me while I keep trying to figure out how to explain what I've been feeling. Too bad there isn't a Dictionary of Jordan J in a library somewhere so that Casey could flip through its pages and figure me out on her own.

She finally stops squinting at me and looks over her shoulder then back at me and then over her shoulder again.

What?
Why is your face doing that?
Hello?
Are we not *cool now?*
Or . . . ?
Is there an alligator behind me or something?

I stand on my tiptoes to get a better look over her shoulder.

I don't see any gators.
Though there is definitely at least one alligator that lives in the pond.
That's why the wildlife people came out and put up that ugly chain-link fence around it.
Even though everyone knows gators can climb fences, you know.

Casey swallows and lets out a pastel-pink laugh and says,

Good to have you back.

She steps closer to me and puts her hands on my shoulders and stares at me with those light brown eyes that don't look like any other eyes that have ever stared at me.

Why does your face say alligator *when you look*
at me, JJ?
It didn't used to do that.
What happened, Jordan?
Why am I an alligator now? What's the real *reason*
you've been hiding from me?

At first I think I'll pretend I really WAS sick and tell her about the barfing and make it sound much worse than it was and then say, *WHEW, GLAD I'M FEELING BETTER NOW* and pretend that everything is super-cool fine okay perfect.

And then I think maybe I won't say anything and I'll grab Ben Hur and run away.

And then I realize I don't want to pretend, and I don't want to run away.

I just don't want to feel this way anymore.

Some words fall out of my mouth and hover in the air between us.

No one should be a clown unless they want
to be an actual clown clown, and then it's okay,
but I don't want to be a clown. Ever.

Casey's forehead and nose crinkle at the same time.

What?
What do you mean?
Who called you a clown?

Ben Hur finishes eating the stick and tries to climb inside Casey's helmet. She's almost small enough to fit. I nudge the helmet with my foot so she has a better angle to give it a whirl. Without looking up, I say,

No one has called me a clown.
I'm just pretty sure they're going to play clown music when I'm on the show.

Casey is extra confused now. She shakes her head.

JJ, I have no idea what you're talking about.

My words come out in a yell.

The show!
When it premieres on TV!
When they show my six out of ten, at best *tryout!*
They're going to play clown music, Casey.
I know they are.
And I wanted to talk to Veronica Verve at callbacks.
To ask her not to do that to me.
But she was always at the judges' table.

And I was never not just-a-kid-in-the-audience watching callbacks.
And just-kids-in-the-audience don't get to talk to judges at the judges' table.
And I'll still be just-a-kid-in-the-audience at finals.
And . . .

I realize I'm yelling and I try to take a deep breath and talk in a regular voice.

I'm not a clown.

Without even one whole second passing, Casey starts yelling right back at me.

Seriously??
SERIOUSLY???????
How is six out of ten *even still in your head???*
You're, like, a million out of ten, JJ!
Without your super-sweet choreography—
Without YOU—
I wouldn't have made it to finals—
WE wouldn't have made it to finals!

Casey's sputters turn to yells just like a dirt bike engine picking up speed.

I won't have a million in ten chance of making it past finals without you.
If you're a clown . . .
If anyone tells you that, or plays clown music at you . . .
Well . . .
You're just going to make being a clown a thing everyone WANTS to be.
I wish I had your talent, JJ.
And I'm lucky that you're sharing it with me.
You're like . . . like . . . the gas to my dirt bike, you know?
I look good . . .

Casey pops her hip and points her chin to the sky.

. . . but I can't jump or fly or even . . . move forward . . . without you.

She points her chin back at me.
She chews her bottom lip.

Her words float in the air between us, wavy, like the heat ripples coming off the pond.

The gas to your dirt bike?
Isn't that a regular you-powered bike right there?
You don't really need gas.

Casey blinks and laughs and breathes out,

Well, yeah, but you get what I'm saying, right?
Without you, my dancing has no spark.
Seriously.
If you're a clown, then you better teach me all your clown moves.

Ben Hur gives up on trying to sleep in Casey's helmet and starts growling and trying to drag me toward whatever mysterious enemy needs her immediate attention and I hope it isn't an alligator.

I say,

I don't know if we have time for you to learn ALL of my clown moves.

Casey rolls her eyes and whacks me on the shoulder.

That's because YOU disappeared for half our practice time!

I say,

Sorry.

Casey says,

My fuel, JJ.
My spark.

I say,

Practice tomorrow?
After school?
Under the tree?

Casey grabs her helmet, stuffs it on her head, and says,

I'll be sure to bring my best clown music, prodigy.

She pedals off in a cloud of dust.

7
6
5
4
3
2

1 DAY(S)

TO FINALS

AFTER SCHOOL AT THE TREE WITH DROOPING BRANCHES

If my life was a movie, the next few days would be one of those scenes where they smush together a bunch of other tiny fast-moving scenes, and there's thumping music and bright colors and the scenes fly by as you watch the main characters working really hard at something, messing up, getting better, messing up again, getting worse, then suddenly WAY better, and THEN . . .

BAM

. . . the fast-moving tiny scenes slow down and it's real life again and now it's time for the main characters to fight the dragon/win the race/rob the bank/ace the test/win the dance competition, whatever.

Casey and I are sweating and tired and sitting under the practice tree drinking warm water from our water bottles and I think our fast-moving scenes are slowing down because Fierce Finals are tomorrow.

> *I can't believe it's already almost time to fight the dragon.*

Casey wipes her mouth with the back of her hand and squints at me like she does when she has no idea what I'm talking about.

Huh? What dragon?
You mean Veronica Verve?

I squint back and look up into the swaying branches of the practice tree.

Did I say that out loud?
Sometimes I don't realize I actually say the things I'm thinking.
Tomorrow IS tomorrow, right?

Casey laughs and shoves me in the shoulder.

For a genius, you sure don't make sense a lot of the time.
Yes, tomorrow is the actual day of actual Fierce Finals.
If that's what you're asking.
Even though it makes me a little bit nervous that you don't know that.

I shove Casey back, and laugh with her.

I DO know that.
Just double-checking.

We sit there for a minute thinking about tomorrow and listening to the rustle of the drooping branches.

My phone buzzes, reminding me that I remembered to bring my phone today.

There's a text from Javi.

> *Shiitake mushrooms.*
> *I'm late AGAIN.*
> *Do you think you can give me a ride to the community center?*

Casey rolls onto her back in the dirt, and throws her arms out to the sides very dramatically.

> *What?*
> *Now?!*
> *It's our last practice!*

I grab one of her hands and drag her to her feet.

> *You're just staring into a tree, Casey.*
> *And you're already at least twenty out of ten outstanding at doing that.*
> *You're also at least twenty out of ten outstanding at dancing this super-sweet routine. Plus, I'll owe you big-time.*

Casey raises one eyebrow.

Owe me what?

She puts a hand on her hip and smiles a half smile like she's posing for the poster of a Disney Channel TV show called *Owe Me What?*

I'll name a dance move after you, how about that?

She laughs.

Tempting, but no.
I need to practice more.
Gotta get everything just right, you know?

I do know.

But also I do NOT know how I'm going to get to old-lady art class for some quality bro time if I don't have a ride over there.

I heave my backpack over my shoulder and wave bye to Casey, who spins and leaps and waves bye back.

OLD-LADY ART CLASS

I'm sorry.

I hate how those are the first words I almost always say when I get to old-lady art class.

I also hate how my words sound a little bit high-pitched and like the kind of whine that comes out of me when I know Mom or Dad is about to punish me no matter what I say.

Tucked into the shadows of his hoodie, Javi's face is scrunched into a point and his arms are crossed tight over his chest and he's not painting and he looks really, really mad.

The Carol(e)s try not to look like they're looking at us, but they're totally looking at us over the birds they're painting.

I try to make my voice sound less whiny but I only succeed in talking in a whisper-whine.

I know I'm late.
But . . .
At least I made it?
We still have some bro time left, right?

Javi gets up and stomps over to the sink and throws away his dirty paint water with a big splash that makes Kat say, *Careful there, Javier.*

Carol clears her throat and she *does* look up at me when she says,

'Bout five minutes, hon.

I guess I look like I don't understand her instead of like I actually feel, which is embarrassed and sad that I made Javi mad.

Carole with an E flicks her head toward the clock at the back of the room and says,

Until class is over.

She flicks her head toward Javi, who's still over by the sinks talking to Kat.

Better get to bro-ing.

They both look back down at their paintings and Carole with an E quietly pushes a package of two pink Snoball snacks at me without looking up.

I take the Snoballs even though they taste like a computer version of strawberries, and I bring them over to Javier and Kat.

Kat smiles when she sees me walking over, and maybe she's the only person in the world besides the Carol(e)s who likes computer-strawberry flavored snacks.

Close but no cigar today, huh?

Huh?

Getting to class?
You missed Paint Your Partner as a
Bird day.

Oh.
Did I?
Sorry.
I'm just—

Javi interrupts me, which he never does, and says a bunch of words in a row, which he barely ever does.

H-he's j-just busy w-with h-his d-d-d-

Javi stops for a second and his face is all mad and scrunched up and I know it's because he hates to stutter in front of people and I know I'm the reason he's probably stressed out AND mad right now.

DANCING.

Javi shouts that last word like he's spitting it into the sink.

When he looks up at me I get an 85% concern that he might start crying and that will make me cry and I don't know if Kat is the kind of grown-up who can deal with more than one crying kid like a Ms. J kind of grown-up could.

I hold out the Snoballs.

> *Finals are tomorrow.*
> *Then it will all be over.*
> *And all my time can be bro time.*

Javi ignores the Snoballs so Kat takes them and opens the package and bites into one, and I KNEW she liked them and that makes me like her less, even though it doesn't make me like the Carol(e)s less, which is interesting and maybe worth thinking about some other time or with Mo if I ever get to see her again.

Kat shakes Snoball crumbs into the sink.

> *What's bro time?*
> *Sounds cool.*

Javi whacks his paintbrushes on the side of the sink, sending wet spatters everywhere and making Kat jump back to protect her Snoballs.

> *It's n-not the* answer *t-to anything,*
> *th-that's f-for s-sure.*

Javi stomps back to our table, leaving Kat with a confused look and a half-eaten Snoball, and me with the kind of sad feeling that makes me want to curl into a Pork Chop Protection Ball™ right here in the middle of the floor.

I curl into a Pork Chop Protection Ball™ in my mind while Kat finishes her Snoball and announces that class is over and she can't wait to see everyone next time.

Javi stomps back to the sinks to finish cleaning his brushes, or maybe just to get away from me, and I'm not sure what to do with myself other than wave bye to the Carol(e)s and say in a way too loud voice,

> *Don't worry, I'm working on a plan to stop being so late every time,*

which is a weird thing for my face to say, because I am not working on that plan at all, but maybe my brain is working on a plan for Javier to hear me say I'm working on a plan so that I will be forced to work on that plan?

The Carol(e)s seem to be working on some kind of plan, too, because they glance at each other and instead of waving bye and walking away from me toward the door, they don't wave at all and walk toward me in an ambush of Carol(e)s.

They corner me on the opposite side of the room from the sinks where Javi is still slamming things around, and they both look at me, frown-smiling.

Carol's voice is quick and quiet as she says,

> *When Javier asked you to spend some bro time creating art with him, maybe the thing he really wanted to create . . .*

Carole with an E interrupts,

> . . . *was* time *with you, Jordan.*

Carol gives her a look as she interrupts back, saying,

> *And maybe the question you should have right now isn't* how *to get to class on time . . .*

Carole with an E interrupts again,

> *. . . but* why *it's so important to Javier to share this bro time with you.*

They each give my elbows a squeeze before they walk off, and . . . hmmm.

I wait for Javi to shove all his supplies into his bag and we don't say anything as we walk outside together.

I hope it's still okay for Javi's mom to give me a ride home, even though I can feel the mad steaming off Javi in big hot waves.

It feels like five hundred silent hours before his mom pulls up and Javi gets in the front seat and I get in the back seat and his mom takes off her sunglasses to get a better look at us.

Hey, you two.
Have fun today?

She turns and looks at me but I look at my lap. I look up just as she looks away and tilts her head at Javi whose eyebrows are pointed in a *V* shape and whose hoodie is pulled up around his ears even though it's five thousand degrees outside.

I'm getting . . .

She looks at me again and she looks at Javi again and then back at me.

. . . a strange vibe.
Everything okay?
Javier?

No one answers and no one says anything about anything for the whole rest of the drive.

I almost ask about the caftan dress covered in clear plastic and hanging from a coat hanger on the other side of the back seat, because it looks just like one of Ms. J's caftans and not at all like the bright white business suits that Javier's mom always wears. But I don't.

Javi turns the radio up and I'm glad it drowns out all the extra-loud silence in the car.

When we get to my house and I climb out of the car, Javi leans over the front seat and shoves a piece of watercolor paper at me and I take it and neither of us says anything and I get out of the car and Javi's mom says, *Bye, Jordan,* and I say, *Thanks for the ride,* and she drives off and I go inside and I think that might have been Javier's last straw with me.

Dad asks about hot dogs or hamburgers for dinner and Mom asks if I'm okay and Carolina asks if I'm going to throw up again and I can't answer anyone because I have no answers for anything because I am not smart like a Carol(e).

JAVIER'S PAINT-YOUR-PARTNER-AS-A-BIRD ASSIGNMENT*

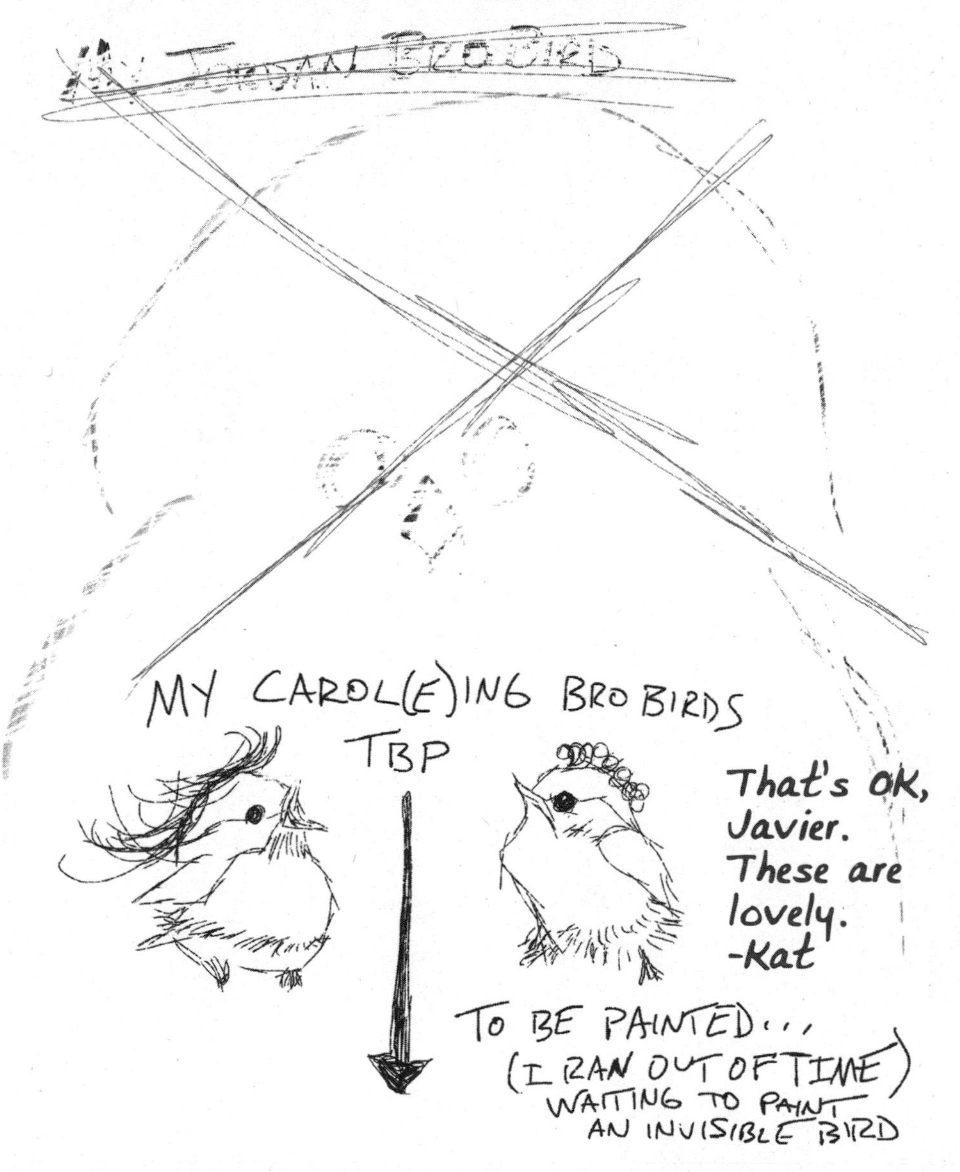

*Burned into my brain in a sticky guilty way that I wish I could rinse out or paint over even though brains don't work like that.

FINALS

INSIDE FRESHWATER'S FAMOUS DING DARLING AUDITORIUM

Casey Price isn't in the bathroom.

She isn't in the other bathroom.

She's not in the audience.

She's not backstage.

She's not in the crowd of dancers comparing ugly feet.

She isn't in line at the check-in table.

She isn't in the snack area.

She's not in the parking lot.

Her *dirt bike* isn't in the parking lot.

She just . . .

isn't here.

I can't call her because she doesn't have a phone.

How did people find each other back in the olden days when everyone was out in the world doing their own thing and no one had a phone in their pocket?

I look in all the places again.

I guess I could call Mom and/or Dad, but I'm not sure how they could help.

A bunch of Rocketeers—who camped out in TENTS all night long to get the first spots in line—run by on their way to grab their seats, and they tell me to break a leg even though I'm not dancing, and they squeal about how excited they are for Casey, and I don't tell them Casey isn't here because none of them can magically call her on her no-phone either, and also I don't want to have to be in the middle of a bunch of Rocketeers all Jordaning along with me.

Out of nowhere I remember the last time I saw Mo and how the clock in her office was counting down the minutes until I'd have to leave without knowing when I'd see her again.

It felt like that clock was sucking out my breath second by second.

I look up at the giant clock in the lobby and feel the same kind of gasps.

I don't know when Casey's number will be called, but it has to be soon.

And if she's not onstage within two minutes of her number being called?

That's a DQ.

Disqualified.

No exceptions.

The DQ music is even worse than the clown music.

STILL INSIDE FRESHWATER'S FAMOUS DING DARLING AUDITORIUM

Maybe Casey has been secretly really really mad at me the past few days?

Because I disappeared on her after callbacks?

And this is her sweet revenge?

STILL INSIDE FRESHWATER'S FAMOUS DING DARLING AUDITORIUM

No way.

Casey wants this just as much as I want it for her. For herself. For me. For both of us.

STILL INSIDE FRESHWATER'S FAMOUS DING DARLING AUDITORIUM

Maybe she's pulling a Jordan and she got her days mixed up.

STILL INSIDE FRESHWATER'S FAMOUS DING DARLING AUDITORIUM

Contestant 0156.
Contestant 0156.
Last call before disqualification.
You have two minutes to get to the stage.

No no no no no no no no no no no no.

I frantically scan the empty lobby.
I run outside and scan more things . . . parking lot, sidewalk, behind the bushes.
I run back inside but there's nothing left to scan.
I can faintly hear the crowd chanting:

Oh-one-five-six!
Oh-one-five-six!
Oh-one-five-six!

The backstage lady with all the eyeliner pushes open the door to backstage with a loud bang that sends my guts into my throat.

She scans the empty lobby just like I did.

She sees me.

Hey, kid.

She squints.

1313?

I nod and run closer to her as she says,

Where's 0156?
She's your dancer, right?
Don't make me tell VV you lost your dancer, kid.

Wha—

Don't look at me like that.
VV has been going on for DAYS about how excited she is to see what you've come up with for 0156.
DAYS, kid.
So . . .

She flings her hands up in a very aggressive shrug.

Go get her!
You've got—

She looks down at her watch and shakes her head.

Thirty-one seconds.
Thirty seconds.
Twenty-nine seconds.
Why aren't you moving?

My legs stop working and I sit down right there on the floor.

I already know I can't find her.
I don't know where she is, but I know she's not here.

The backstage lady's eyeballs go back and forth a bunch of times like she's trying to roll them back in her head to find words to say to me. She says a swear and then in a voice I think she thinks I can't hear, she grunts:

I can not be lieve this.

Neither can I, Backstage Lady.

Just as the backstage door is about to slam shut behind her, she pushes it open again and says,

Get over here, 1313.
Now.

I jump up and run over to her and my mouth opens to be like *WHA—HUH?*, but she flings her palm up in my face.

Follow me and don't say one word.

STILL INSIDE FRESHWATER'S FAMOUS DING DARLING AUDITORIUM, BUT IN THE ACTUAL AUDITORIUM PART WITH THE CHANTING CROWD AND THE JUDGES' TABLE

I follow the backstage lady up a bunch of stairs and past some giant guys who are maybe security guards, and past some other people holding very fancy TV cameras, and we weave our way through the empty seats that turn the judges' table into a little oasis in this rocking ocean of chanting audience people.

The backstage lady tells me NOT TO MOVE and she leaves me standing about four seats away from the judges' table and I watch her hand cover the skinny microphone that sticks up from the table in front of Veronica Verve while she leans over and whispers into Veronica Verve's ear.

Veronica Verve's hair is very white and very spiky and her face is also very spiky when she whips around to look at me.

Her spiky face softens a little bit and she waves me over.

I would be so so so excited about Veronica Verve waving me over if I wasn't so so so worried about Casey disappearing out of nowhere. Into nowhere?

I walk closer and Veronica Verve stares at me for what feels like a very long time. I'm so close I can smell how she smells and it's like fruit and sweat and something spiky. She leans back in her chair just as Mae Michaelson leans forward in her chair. They both stare at me. It's Mae who talks first.

> *You're the one who choreographed those blistering moves at prelims, yeah? And that brilliantly explosive callback routine?*

I nod because I can't find any words.

Veronica Verve looks at me and her expression is very serious, like this is the most serious of all serious moments that ever serioused.

> *So, where's your dancer, prodigy?*

I am pretty sure I'm about to cry a lot and probably kind of loudly, so I keep not saying anything and instead I shrug.

Mae Michaelson shakes her head.

> *Wow, kid.*
> *Just . . . wow.*
> *Way to blow up the biggest opportunity you might ever have ha—*

Veronica Verve reaches over and dumps Mae's drink in her lap.

Wait.
What.
Did she really just—

Instead of a loud weep, I strangle out a surprised laugh.

Mae jumps up and swears and yells for a towel. A bunch of people run around trying to find her a towel while Veronica Verve's very serious face turns into a soft smile that doesn't match her loud voice.

She snaps in the direction of a person dressed all in black who's wearing an earbud like one of those people who protect the president of the United States. They whisper and nod.

Veronica Verve stands up and stretches her neck from side to side, never not looking at me.

I want you to walk me through it.

At first I'm not sure she's talking to me, but she's looking at me without blinking, so that helps me figure out that yes, she's talking to me, but not what exactly she's talking *about*.

I say,

Walk you through it?

And she says,

Yeah.
Walk me through your new routine.

Veronica Verve takes off her sweater, kicks off her shoes, and bounces down into a stretch.

I want to see what you have up your sleeve, prodigy.

She winks at me and instead of squealing or fainting or having sixteen heart attacks, I say,

Are you sure you've got it in you?

WHY WOULD I EVEN SAY THAT WHO DO I THINK I AM?

The audience goes,

Oooooooooohhhhhh.

And I had forgotten there even *was* an audience for a minute there.

Even Mae Michaelson laughs out loud in a surprised hoot.

Veronica Verve shakes her head at me, but she's smiling big while she stretches.

Hit me with what you got, prodigy.

So I take a deep breath and I do.

I explain all the moves and how they work together, and I tell her when Casey pops big and when she goes small and Veronica Verve listens and nods and tries a few of the moves I invented myself just to make sure she understands what I mean, and then she runs down all the stairs and I run down after her and a camera lady runs down after me.

Veronica Verve climbs up onstage, like literally climbs up the front of the stage, swings around on her booty, jumps to her feet, yells *OH-ONE-FIVE-SIX MUSIC CUE GO*, and then right there, in front of the whole audience and the TV cameras and everyone . . .

Veronica Verve dances my blistering choreography.

When she finishes, the crowd explodes into the loudest cheering I've ever heard.

Veronica Verve bows and then motions to me, and the spotlight finds me and everyone claps and cheers and I'm smiling so big it hurts my face.

I yell up to the stage,

Pretty good, but you're no Casey Price.

Mae Michaelson yells,

I give it a six out of ten, great effort.

Veronica shakes her fist at us, but she's laughing when she hops off the stage. She throws her arm around me just as the audience bursts into more cheers and hoots and applause.

The backstage lady walks out onstage and yells,

Okay, everyone, let's take ten before the next round of dancers hits the stage.

Veronica Verve squeezes my shoulders before she lets go and laughs and shout-says,

Not as good as Casey Price, huh?
Is that 0156's name?

That's when a thought slithers down my spine like cold rain.

STILL STANDING NEXT TO VERONICA VERVE IN FRONT OF THE STAGE IN FRESHWATER'S FAMOUS DING DARLING AUDITORIUM

OMG.

MAYBE CASEY PRICE *ACTUALLY DID* CRASH HER DIRT BIKE AND SHE *ACTUALLY IS* INJURED IN A DITCH SOMEWHERE.

INSIDE A SMALL ROOM IN FRESHWATER'S FAMOUS DING DARLING AUDITORIUM

I take a sip of the cold bubbly water Veronica Verve gave me just after she sat me down in this room and just before she walked out very quickly, leaving me in here all by myself.

Then Veronica Verve pushes her way back into the room with one of the security guards and kneels by my side.

How are you feeling, prodigy?
You spaced out there, huh?
Kinda fainted with your eyes open?
Or . . . I don't even know?

I've never fainted before, but sometimes if the Jordan-ing gets intense enough I can't hear people talking to me until I snap out of it.

Veronica Verve keeps talking in a voice that's more deep and forceful than loud. I like this volume better.

Are you here with anyone?
An adult, I mean?
Richard will go find them if you give me their name.

My face must do a thing because she pats my knee and says,

Do you want Richard to get a medic?

She shoots her laser eyes at Richard.

I told you to bring a medic!

I manage to squeak out a *No* and a bubbly water burp at the same time.

I can feel my body wanting to pull itself into a Pork Chop Protection Ball™.

My parents aren't here.
My mom dropped me off this morning.

Someone knocks on the door, and the security guard guy, Richard, opens it and I breathe out a long breath when I see Ms. Masterson standing there in her turquoise track suit.

Ms. Masterson?
What are you *doing here?*

Ms. Masterson puts her hands on her hips.

I am the artistic director of the Hart Rocketeers dance team.
Why wouldn't *I be here?*

I shake my head.

No.
I mean here *here.*
In this tiny room.

Ms. Masterson takes a deep breath and closes her eyes and opens them again and says,

I was leaving when I saw them escort you over here.
Casey's brother called me a few minutes ago.
I'm on my way to see her.
Would you like to come with me?

I jump up and spill my bubbly water everywhere.

Over where?
Is Casey okay?!
She's not injured in a ditch somewhere, right?!

Ms. Masterson says,

She's not in a ditch.
She IS at the hospital, though.
If you'd like to come with me, we should go.

Veronica Verve stands up and puts her hands on her hips.

Security Guard Richard looks at Veronica Verve and then at Ms. Masterson and then at me.

> *That okay with you, kid?*
> *You know this woman?*
> *She telling the truth?*

I say,

> *Yes, I know her.*
> *She's a teacher so I think she HAS to tell the truth?*

I don't say the other thing I'm thinking which is that I *am* a little bit worried about riding in a car with her because she might spend the whole time yelling at me for taking away Casey as her private dance student, and also for writing my Boo-Yah Reports.

Ms. Masterson tries to smile at me in a nice way which looks a little bit like she has a stomachache.

> *It's okay, Jordan.*
> *I know you think I hate you, but I promise I don't.*
> *You're a very talented young man . . . with a very poison pen.*
> *We can talk about that at a later date.*
> *Right now we need to make our way to Casey.*
> *Okay?*
> *Why don't you call your mom and tell her what's going on.*

I say *Okay* even though I don't really know what's going on.

Veronica Verve yells:

WAIT!

in her loud stage voice and grabs some paper off a table and starts writing really fast.

We wait even though Casey is IN THE HOSPITAL AND WE NEED TO GO.

Veronica Verve finally hands me two folded up notes.

One for you.
One for Casey.
Go find your dancer, prodigy.
And sometime in the future, come find me.
Deal?
We have more to talk about.

Deal! I can make a list if you want, of things to talk about. Like super-sweet dance moves and no more clown music unless it involves actual clown-related dance vision and—

Ms. Masterson grabs my arm and drags me off while Veronica Verve waves and laughs.

THINGS I NEVER EXPECTED TO SEE OR HEAR OR TALK ABOUT IN MS. MASTERSON'S CAR: A LIST BY JORDAN J

1. more empty bags from Fran's than in Dad's car
2. a conversation about the pros and cons of dirt bikes
3. a conversation about the pros and cons of school newspapers
4. how we both think Casey Price is the best dancer we've ever met
5. sometimes Ms. Masterson checks on Casey at her house because it can be *a very chaotic environment*
6. Casey's brother Paul was a Rocketeer when HE went to Hart Middle School a million years ago
7. Paul is Casey's legal guardian
8. a legal guardian is a person who acts like your parents but isn't technically a parent
9. that's why Paul was the one who called Ms. Masterson
10. how awesome Veronica Verve's hair is

FRESHWATER GENERAL HOSPITAL EMERGENCY ROOM

Ms. Masterson and I walk through the sliding-glass doors that say EMERGENCY on them and I feel a 99% concern that I might try to hold her hand because I am that scared of being in the emergency room even if it isn't because I'm the one who's hurt.

I try to take a deep cleansing breath but out of nowhere Ms. Masterson shouts, *Paul!* right by my ear and I don't know why she's yelling but I *do* know she knows my name isn't Paul, so . . .

I take one step away from Ms. Masterson in case she shouts someone else's name at me again and that's when I see a tall man with a long beard and Casey's same brown eyes walking really fast toward us from far down a hallway on the other side of the waiting room.

He's holding two sodas that I bet you a million dollars are going to explode when he opens them because he is pretty much jogging toward us now.

Sheila.

The man with the beard—*Paul?*—hugs Ms. Masterson—*Sheila?*—and he says,

She's right down here.

They both start walking superfast toward a different hallway and I hype some leaps to keep up.

> *Hello?*
> *Hi?*
> *I'm Jordan.*
> *Are you Casey's brother?*
> *Is Casey okay?*

He's walking so fast that he's two hyper leaps ahead of us now and he doesn't answer my questions, but maybe that's because he didn't hear them over the very loud *swish swish* of Ms. Masterson's tracksuit pants as we speed-walk to catch up.

We pass by beeps and smells that I do not like.

We pass by curtains that don't really hide the people behind them and people wearing gowns that don't really hide anything either.

Finally, Paul pushes his way past a curtain at the end of the hall.

Ms. Masterson follows him.

I start to follow her but then I stop because I'm afraid of what beeps and smells might be behind this curtain and I'm even more afraid that they will make me afraid of Casey and I don't want to be afraid of her or her beeps or smells.

Ms. Masterson sticks her head around the curtain.

Jordan?

I try to blink away my incoming Jordan-ing.

Ms. Masterson walks all the way around the curtain now and stands in front of me and looks into my eyes.

I know hospitals are a little . . . alarming.

She pokes me with her elbow and her laugh sounds more like a snort, and what? Ms. Masterson thinks she's a comedian or something?

I smile a tiny bit mostly out of surprise that Ms. Masterson is trying to be funny and nice instead of whistle-y and scary.

Casey is going to be just fine.
She really wants to see you.

Ms. Masterson holds out a hand and I might have had a 99% concern about wanting to hold her hand when we walked into the emergency room, but now I have a 99% concern that Casey Price will see me holding her hand and make fun of me forever so I put my hand on Ms. Masterson's shoulder instead and follow her past the curtain.

CASEY'S ROOM* IN THE EMERGENCY ROOM

For one tiny blip of a second I feel so relieved to see Casey alive and smiling and sitting up in the hospital bed drinking a soda I'm afraid I might have to curl up into a Pork Chop Protection Ball™ to protect myself from all my own feelings flying at me.

But then my relief squeals to a stop and I feel prickles up and down my arms, all the tiny hairs standing up and shivering at once.

Casey's leg is wrapped in a hot-pink cast almost all the way up to her hip.

She has a white bandage taped to the side of her head where some of her hair has been shaved off.

She has an IV tube connected to one arm.

I don't know why, but I start to say, *It's okay. It's okay. It's okay.*

Ms. Masterson's eyes fly to me, and she whispers around her hand, *This is why I hate dirt bikes.*

Casey gulps her soda, looks straight at me, and says in a strangly voice,

*Not really a room, just an . . . area . . . with a bed and a chair and a table and a curtain.

You were right about alligators, Jordan.
They CAN *climb fences.*

Her brother's eyes get so big I can see the whites all the way around, then they squint just like Casey's do, and he gently whacks her on the shoulder.

Not cool.
This kid is already scared half to death.
Be nice.

Half of Casey's mouth kind of smiles.

It's a better story, though.

Ms. Masterson sits in a chair next to Casey's bed and crosses her arms and looks like she really wishes she had a whistle to blow.

So, what's the actual story?

I point at Ms. Masterson.

Yeah. What she said.

Casey's brother shakes his head.

You want to tell them?
Or do you want me to tell them?

He doesn't wait for Casey to answer, though. He just keeps talking.

This ding-dong thought it was a great idea to SELL
her dirt bike.
The dirt bike that used to be mine, by the way.
And then she bought some cheap used mountain bike
to replace it.

THEN the ding-dong tried to ride the cheap used
mountain bike on a DIRT BIKE PATH.
Excuse me, not just ride it on the dirt bike path, but
ride it over some jumps.

Guess what happens when a ding-dong tries to jump
a cheap mountain bike like it's an actual dirt bike?

He crosses his arms and nods at Casey's leg and points a finger at her head.

THAT happens.

Casey sighs,

This *happens.*

My brain puzzles together a question.

> *Why would you sell your dirt bike?*
> *You love that thing.*
> I *love that thing.*
> *It's awesome.*

Paul looks at me for maybe the first time since I got here and he nods and says,

> *It IS awesome, right?*
> *Or at least it was.*

Casey sets her soda on a little side table and gives me a very intense *duh* look.

> *I love dancing, JJ.*
> *And I want to be awesome.*

Her brother snorts,

> *Bizarre way of coming at THAT goal.*

Casey says,

> *Shut up, Paul.*

And then,

> *I needed to pay you for your dance vision, JJ.*
> *So I could be awesome.*
> *And get on the show.*

Wait.
What?

> *But . . . I thought you were paying me the money that was supposed to be for your private lessons with Ms. Masterson.*

It's Ms. Masterson's turn to sputter out, *What?! I don't teach private lessons!*

Then everyone is talking at once but I very quickly realize that I don't care what anyone is saying; I just care that Casey is mostly fine and not lying in a ditch somewhere.

A nurse comes in and tells us that we're being too loud and need to go to the waiting room, and Paul and Ms. Masterson noisily leave and I quietly stay behind so I can talk to Casey alone for a second.

I stand by the curtain so it looks like I'm about to leave in case the nurse comes back to yell at me for not leaving yet.

I would have done it for free, you know.

Casey smiles and says,

I know.
But I didn't want *you to do it for free.*
I wanted you to know how much I . . .

She looks up and hunts around for the right word before looking back at me.

valued . . .
your super-sweet dance moves.
Does that make sense?

I don't really know what to say to that, so I pull the letter from Veronica Verve out of my pocket and hand it to her.

Speaking of super-sweet things—

As she reads the note, Casey's eyes get bigger and bigger and her mouth falls open and she looks up at me and goes,

Whaaaaa—!
Did you read this?

I try to pretend I didn't but my face gives me away.

Casey laughs and swats at me, but her swat is very limited because of the IV tube.

Did you get one, too?

I nod.

Can I see it?

I nod again and hand it to her and my cheeks feel just as pink as the cast on her leg.

FIERCE ACROSS AMERICA

Dear Casey, aka 0156,

Sorry you missed finals, kid. It appears to have been an emergency, and for that, I'm truly sorry. I hope you and your family are okay. You're one of the best dancers I've seen this year, and I've seen a LOT of dancers.

Keep practicing.

I'll see you at Season 16 callbacks. You can skip prelims next time.

BRING THIS NOTE.

x,

VV

VV

FIERCE ACROSS AMERICA

Dear JJ,

I don't want to see you at auditions next year, you hear me? You're already too good for this show, prodigy. Trust.

Your next step is to find a performing-arts high school and go there. Listen and learn, but never let anyone try to tame you. Your instinct is fire, kid. It's pure energy. Add a little training to that natural talent, and BOO-YAH. You're gonna electrify the dance world, JJ.

They might even start calling you Veronica Verve II. Ha!

Keep in touch.

x,

VV

VV

PS: Let me know if you need a letter of recommendation or help finding a scholarship.

Casey looks up at me.

Um.
That's a ten out of ten outstanding letter.

I grin.

Yours is pretty good, too.

Casey pretends to frown.

I mean . . . it's like . . . a six out of ten?
At best?

That's when I remember that I haven't told her ANYTHING about what happened at finals, so I move away from the curtain and sit in the chair next to her bed and steal a sip of her soda and launch into the whole story even though I know I'll be loud and the nurse will come back to yell at me.

AFTER FINALS

THINGS TO SAY TO JAVIER WHEN WE STOP BY HIS HOUSE: A LIST BY JORDAN J

1. I'm sorry for not taking the time part of our bro time seriously
2. I'm really really sorry about that
3. I hope you know you're my best bro even when I do things that make it hard for you to believe me
4. I will understand if Carol and Carole with an E are your new bros now
5. I painted this Javier bird for you ——→ (turn paper over)
6. if you stop being mad at me, we can have nonstop bro time at my house
   a. my parents already said it was okay
   b. I won't make you watch old *Fierce Across America* episodes like usual
7. I really am sorry

My friend Javi as a bird

by Jordan J

hoodie
even though it's hot
all the time

*

heart because
he's so nice and
cares about
everyone,
even his bro
Jordan J
(me) (even
when he's
mad he's
still a good
and nice
friend.)

smile
because
Javi likes
to smile
and laugh

notepad because
he's always drawing
awesome things.

* sorry your beak is so weird, Javi, it's really
hard to make beaks with watercolors.
Your beak is very nice irl. Ha Ha.

JAVIER'S HOUSE

Hey, Jordan.
Come on in.

Javier's mom hops back onto the couch with some other lady, who's facing the TV and yelling at sports guys doing sports-guy things.

Javi's mom twists around on the couch so she can see me still standing by the front door and she smiles at me in a way that reminds me of how someone smiles at you when they tell you not to run around a swimming pool and then you run anyway and you slip and fall and skin your knee, but they're nice enough to give you a bag of ice and not say *I told you so.*

Javi's in his room.

I walk down the hallway and look at all the pictures hanging on the wall. Every single one is a picture of Javi as a baby or a tiny kid and he's smiling in every single picture.

When I walk through his open bedroom door and see him on his stomach on his bed drawing in a notebook, he is not smiling.

I put my list on the bed in front of him.

He doesn't look up and he doesn't look at the list and he doesn't say anything and he doesn't smile so I sigh and walk out of his room and wave bye to his mom, and the other lady yells, *You have to catch the ball and THEN run!*

My brain does a confusing swirl as I walk out of the house and climb into Mom's car because that lady's voice sounded really familiar, almost like Ms. J yelling, *We don't RUN in the library!*

Wait.

< Not Newspaper Typing Club Chat >

jajajavier:): What are you doing?

JORDANJMAGEDDON!!!!: I'm trying to use fairies to build a giant Javi Bro-Bird in the sky.

JORDANJMAGEDDON!!!!: They're really mean, though.

jajajavier:): Yeah, they are. You should be wearing armor.

jajajavier:): Also, why are you using fairies to build a giant Me Bro-Bird in the sky?

JORDANJMAGEDDON!!!!: So I can show you that I'm sorry. 😟

jajajavier:): I don't know if that makes any sense, but okay.

jajajavier:): Do you need some help?

JORDANJMAGEDDON!!!!: Javi!

JORDANJMAGEDDON!!!!: You can't help make your own apology sky bird!

jajajavier:): Who says?

JORDANJMAGEDDON!!!!: Me says. I says.

JORDANJMAGEDDON!!!!: Javi?

jajajavier:): Yeah?

JORDANJMAGEDDON!!!!: Did you want to have bro time so you could talk to me about the lady watching sports on your couch w

CHAT INFRACTION

JORDANJMAGEDDON!!!!: your couch, who sounds a lot like Ms. J?

jajajavier:): Maybe.

JORDANJMAGEDDON!!!!: WAS that Ms. J? 😳
JORDANJMAGEDDON!!!!: In your house? 😳 😳 😳

jajajavier:): Maybe.

JORDANJMAGEDDON!!!!: Do you want to talk about it now?

jajajavier:): No.
jajajavier:): I wanted to talk about it during old-lady art class bro time.
jajajavier:): I wanted time to talk about a lot of things, actually.

JORDANJMAGEDDON!!!!: Sorry.

jajajavier:): You didn't know.

JORDANJMAGEDDON!!!!: If I was smart like a Carol(e) I would've known.
JORDANJMAGEDDON!!!!: But I know now.

jajajavier:): You're smart like a Jordan J, which is all I care about.
jajajavier:): Maybe I can come over and we can not watch Fierce Across America?

JORDANJMAGEDDON!!!!: And we can not watercolor?

jajajavier:): And we can just hang out?
jajajavier:): And eat ice cream?

JORDANJMAGEDDON!!!!: And feel some feelings about all the things that have been happening lately?

jajajavier:): Sounds exactly like the bro time I've been waiting for.

JORDANJMAGEDDON!!!!: Should we invite the Carol(e)s? 🤔

jajajavier:): ja ja ja
jajajavier:): Maybe next time.

THINGS TO REMEMBER TO TALK TO MO ABOUT WHEN I FINALLY GET TO SEE HER AGAIN, WHICH WILL BE REALLY REALLY SOON OR AT LEAST AS SOON AS MOM FINDS A PARKING SPOT: A LIST BY JORDAN J

1. uh
2. I know there has to be a lot of stuff
3. how come I can't remember anything?
4. why does this ALWAYS HAPPEN?
5. maybe I should just show her all the notes and lists and stuff that are squished in the bottom of my backpack
6. where is my backpack

MO'S OFFICE

I look at Mo, who is sitting across from me with all my lists and letters on top of the notebook on her lap.

She looks over her glasses at me.

> *You wrote all of this since the last time we talked?*

I try to make my face look like her face and my voice sound like her voice.

> *Well, hasn't it been at least one million years since I was here?*

Mo flips through the papers again and then she looks up at me and raises her eyebrows.

> *Hasn't it been only one month?*

I raise my eyebrows back at her and say,

> *Hasn't it really been one million years* smushed into *one month?*

Mo gives me that Mo look that I've missed so much and she says,

> *Would you like to say more about that?*

And for the first time maybe in my whole life, I have so much to say, I don't know how to start saying it.

So I say it with dance moves instead of words.

And for just a minute I have all the answers.
And for just a minute everything makes perfect sense.

THE HART TIMES

★ ★ ★ *JORDAN J'S* ★ ★ ★

BOO-YAH REPORT #4!

Here's the thing: The Hart Rocketeers dance team is about to be REALLY good. Not only is Casey Price on the mend, but yours truly, Jordan J (no relation to Ms. J) has just become assistant artistic director.

How can this amazingly miraculous miracle be true, you might wonder?

Well, it's a long story, but the TLDR version is that Ms. Masterson hates the Freshwater North Fire 'Canes more than she hates me.

Also, we agreed that she can fire me if the Fire 'Canes beat us at the district competition later this year.

Also, as an apology for all the things I said in all the other reports, I am picking up all the dog poop in her yard for a month.

I have a theory: The Hart Rocketeers will definitely win at Districts because they are dedicated and talented

★ ★ ★ ★ ★

dancers who are hungry to win. Also they really like yelling *PRODIGYYYYY* when I walk in the gym, so that might actually be the only reason I have this new job now, other than Ms. Masterson needing help with her gross backyard.

Either way, BOO-YAH REPORT OUT!

Dance like EVERYONE'S watching,

Jordan J

Jordan,
This is really excellent work.
I have NO NOTES!!!
Boo-yah!
—Ms J

CONGRA

Shout out to C

FIERCE ACROSS AMERICA

★★★★★